KASUBA'S INNER SAFARI QUEST

A Journey of Self-Discovery & Overcoming Your Fears by Being True to Yourself

Enjoy the read!

KASUBA'S INNER SAFARI QUEST

A Journey of Self-Discovery & Overcoming Your Fears by Being True to Yourself

Bwalya Penza

Published by Author Academy Elite
PO Box 43, Powell, OH 43065
www.AuthorAcademyElite.com

Interior Illustrations: Chichi-René Chona

Identifiers:
LCCN: 2021900287
ISBN: 978-1-64746-669-5 (paperback)
ISBN: 978-1-64746-670-1 (hardback)
ISBN: 978-1-64746-671-8 (ebook)

Available in paperback, hardback, e-book, and audiobook

This book is dedicated to my sister-child Chichi-René, my *papillon*, my bug, my number one hype-man and cheerleader; my *kasuba, mwezi*, and *lutanda* (sun, moon, and star).

***

To Chaila, *'The Little Bro'* you stayed true to yourself from your very first sunrise to your very last sunset. This one's for you!

CONTENTS

PART 6. RECOGNITION

FOREWORD

This is a wonderful story! I love how Bwalya uses her coaching hat to turn a safari story into a self-help novel for kids.

The self-help intros to each part of the story are great. Since kids may not always be able to read into a deeper meaning of stories, this gives them a frame of reference with which to view the piece of the story they're about to read.

It's relevant to modern times as it shows the main character dealing with the home schooling that many kids are struggling with today. Kids will be able to relate to Kasuba on a powerful level.

The word "Safari" conjures up so many great images for kids: vacation, animals, adventure, and maybe a slight bit of danger because they might be exploring something unknown. Not only will this self-help novel guide them through their everyday challenges, but it will engage them with a fun and entertaining read.

The reflections really tie up the lesson from each story. The structure put together is really strong and helps kids relate the story to what's going on in their lives.

This book can be read by kids independently, but it also lends itself well to discussion, therefore being a great acquisition for any school, parent, or educator. This book can be used to help children struggling with issues around change and belief in themselves, helping them find their place in the world.

—Renaye Thornborrow
Founder of Adventures in Wisdom® and leader of a
worldwide movement to empower kids
https://adventuresinwisdom.com/

ACKNOWLEDGMENTS

I would like to thank the very many children I have come across throughout my coaching career and before. You have helped nurture the inner child within. A huge thank you goes to my daughter, Chichi-René, my nephews, Kocha and Nebu, and my niece, Niara (KP!), whose characters are sprinkled throughout this tale. I would like to thank my mother, Chibulu Jane, for nurturing my love for books and stories. Thanks to my brothers, Ntazana (the big bro) and Chaila (the little bro), for their love and support.

I thank my small mummy, Mummy Chanda, for helping me out with all the Bemba sayings and ensuring I spelt them correctly.

A big thank you to my other hype-man, my all-weather friend and sister, Nankhonde Kasonde Van den Broek.

I give very special thanks to my *first born,* Banji-Rae, and my sister-friends, Elizabeth (Sumiya) Nkhoma & Anna Musonda Phiri, for reading this manuscript, for your amazing feedback, and for your love and support.

My big-little sister, Kessy-La, thank you for bringing me up to speed on wildlife crime prevention and making sure I did not misrepresent the great work that's been done to stop poaching and crime on wildlife.

To my mentor for the past year, Samhita Rao, thank you for your encouragement and advice while I juggled writing this book with growing my children's coaching business.

My *Veuve-sister,* Catherine Ndashe Phiri, thank your for providing an avenue to help me build and strengthen both my writing and coaching muscles through my article contributions in SKY Magazine.

Thank you to Renaye Thornborrow and my entire Adventures in Wisdom® family for all the work you do empowering children throughout the world.

A huge thank you to all the game rangers, guides, spotters, and scouts in the national parks that I have visited since childhood: Kafue National Park, Kasanka National Park, Lochinvar National Park, Lower Zambezi National Park, Mosi-oa-Tunya National Park, Nsumbu National Park and of course South Luangwa National Park (Mfuwe Lodge & Chinzombo).

I am so grateful for Author Academy Elite; you're such an amazing team and family. I particularly want to thank Tina Morlock for your faith and belief in this story. Extra-special thanks go out to my super fabulous editor, Felicity Fox, for your guidance, your patience, and your grace.

Finally, to my soul-sister, Shimbs, thank you for bringing 'The Course' into my life:

'By grace I live. By grace I am released.
By grace I give. By grace I will release'[1]

SAFARI SUNRISE—A NOTE TO PARENTS, MENTORS, AND EDUCATORS

If you have been on a safari before, you may recall the conflicting emotions you experienced before, during, and after the safari—excitement, fear, overwhelm, anxiety, then humbled. Whether or not you've been on a safari, the journey of life is very similar. You go through ups and downs, calm and quiet introspection moments, and scary and fun moments too.

Sometimes, you are pleasantly surprised but disappointed at other times—you didn't get to see the leopard this time. In life—or a safari—your presence and authenticity guide your experience. A safari at sunrise is very different from one at sunset. During the morning safari, some animals are easier to spot, and some use their surroundings to camouflage themselves. However, on the evening safari, the guide uses a spotlight to guide your eyes towards the game. In the same way, you have an inner compass navigating you through life.

Kasuba is a twelve-year-old girl uprooted from everything familiar—friends, school, home, and extended family—to live in a game park seemingly in the middle of nowhere. Her mobile phone hardly ever has any signal, so she can't even watch her favourite TV shows. She's going through this without the two friends she's known all her life—Zozo, her dog, and Sekai, her best friend.

Like many other children, Kasuba faces several challenges but learns to embrace life's changes by trusting and letting her inner voice guide her. She takes us on a journey with wild animals and poachers and new friends and enemies. The journey seems so far removed from her life, but it soon mirrors her path. She learns the laws of the wilderness while learning some very important life lessons. Join Kasuba on her safari, and she'll help your children open their eyes to how they can confidently navigate their way through life and obstacles during their transformation from child to teen/young adult. Kasuba will help children through decision making, developing self-esteem and self-confidence, and ultimately, being true to themselves.

PART 1
RUMINATION

Rumination *noun*

The act of thinking deeply about something; deep thoughts about something.[2]

CHAPTER 1
HOW DID I GET HERE?

D o you ever feel like everyone except you has a say in what happens in your life? And do you feel powerless, like you have to go with the flow, and whatever *you* want doesn't matter?

Newsflash! You're not alone. We all go through this at some point in our lives, and for a lot of adults, it happens many times over. The great news for you, though, is life doesn't have to be like this. Unlike your parents and the many adults you know, you get to discover this now so you can do something about it. Don't worry; this is all new to me as well. Come on safari with me, and I'll show you exactly what I mean!

* * *

The plane landed with a thud and jolted me awake. For a brief moment, I forgot where I was. I gazed out the window from my seat on the British Aerospace Jetstream 41—that's what the safety card says. My mum, dad, and annoying little brother, Mwezi, sat with me. We landed at the airstrip in Mfuwe, and I heard the pilot's voice over the intercom, apologising for the rough landing. My mum's job transferred her here—she was an animal conservationist. I don't understand why they brought me along. Her stupid job turned my whole life upside down. It's so loud in this stupid plane; how could anyone hear themselves think? I hate my mum and her stupid job, and I hate my dad for making me go. Mwezi thought this was some big adventure, so he was no help. He bounced up and down in his chair, excited. Stupid kid!

Parents are the worst; my mbuya (grandma) said I could stay with her, but my parents said no. It's like they enjoyed making my life miserable. Mbuya lived alone because my shikulu (grandpa) died long before I was born. She said I reminded her of him. A rhinoceros killed Shikulu in the bush while he tried to save it from poachers. Poachers break the law by hunting and killing endangered animals, but also, they do not have a license to hunt the animals. Poor poachers hunt kudu and antelope to feed their families, but cruel poachers kill leopards and rhinos to sell their skin and horns. I've never understood why anyone would want a leopard skin or a rhino horn, but there are some crazy people out there. Unfortunately, those crazy people lived where our new home was! I mean, the place was so dangerous; they wouldn't even let me bring Zozo! They said he might run away from the camp and get eaten by a lion. How come they weren't worried about lions eating *us*? *Stupid job in a stupid camp where stupid lions eat people's dogs, and stupid rhinos kill people's shikulus!*

When they opened the plane door, it was like someone had transported us to the Sahara Desert. The heat was insane; I've never felt anything like it. While still on the plane, my mum already wiped the sweat off her forehead and neck with her handkerchief made of small, golden yellow sunflowers. It never got that hot in Lusaka. *I really missed home.*

Some guy named Peter met us at the airport. He worked at the camp and was so excited to see my parents. From the way they talked, it sounded like they grew up together. Like my mum, Peter also worked with animals. He brought us ice-cold bottles of water.

'Thank you, next,' I said.

'K, that's rude; you know better. Apologise!' my mum snapped.

My mum usually called me Bug, as in her travel bug, because ever since I was little, she's taken me on so many local and international trips. When she called me K, I knew she was unhappy with me.

Mwezi burst out laughing. 'It's that song she's always singing. Thank you! Next, next,' he sang off-key.[3]

'I don't care what it's from! It's very rude, and she knows better,' my mother snapped back.

'I'm sorry,' I said to Peter, biting the inside of my lip.

'There's the face that lights up the whole of the Luangwa Valley! You really look like your grandfather,' he said with a smile.

No one ever talked about Shikulu, except for Mbuya. 'You knew my grandpa?' I asked.

'Of course! Everything I know, I learned from him. Your mum and I grew up like siblings, and your shikulu was like a father to me. We all called him ba Tata and your mbuya— who we call ba Mayo—made the best tripe stew I ever tasted,' he said.

'Well, ba Mayo must have known you were craving her cooking because she delivered a container of ichifu (tripe) for you this morning,' my mum said to Peter.

'I don't believe it! That's a woman after my heart! You see, Kasuba, ba Mayo still feeds me, even after all these years,' Peter said with a huge smile on his face and rubbed his tummy. He looked genuinely excited about eating the boiled stomach lining of a cow.

'Tripe stew! *Ichifu*! Yucky!' Mwezi said while making a face like he had just swallowed some imaginary tripe stew.

My dad looked at Mwezi, unamused.

'I see you're the Moon to your sister's Sun,' Peter said to Mwezi.

'Yes, that's us—the Sun and the Moon, but I shine much brighter than my sister; she's a grump-a-saurus,' Mwezi said, making roaring dinosaur sounds. I completely ignored him.

'And there's your mother, *Lutanda,* the star. Your dad has a complete natural navigation system at his fingertips!' Peter said, looking very pleased with himself, like he was the first person to ever make that connection with our names.

'Peter actually introduced me to your mum,' my dad chimed in.

'He and your mum were inseparable. I thought they were boyfriend and girlfriend. You know, like you and Sekai.'

'Eww, Dad! You know Kai isn't my boyfriend!' I said.

My parents laughed, but I didn't find any of it funny. Mwezi started singing, 'Kay and Kai, sitting in the tree K – I – S – S – I – N – G!'

I put on my earphones to drown out his annoying voice. Great. 8% battery. I wondered if the day could get any worse.

As we walked towards the minivan, I thought about my shikulu—the man I never met but constantly heard we shared a striking resemblance. Then, I heard the predictable phrase, 'You should've been a boy! You look *just like* your grandfather.' The only person who spoke about him was Mbuya, but she talked about how much he loved the animals and how it ultimately killed him. She said he spent more time with those animals than with people, but they still turned on him. I only really had her perspective; everyone else got too sad when his name came up.

Maybe Peter had interesting stories about him or my mum and dad when they were kids. My dad grew up in the bush, but he never talked about it. Mbuya said he and Shikulu were close, so it was difficult for him to talk about the bush or how he grew up because everything reminded him of Grandpa. My paternal grandfather was still alive, but my dad doesn't have a great relationship with him. He was closer to my shikulu. It's weird, but they all grew up together, so I didn't understand why he agreed when Mum told him about her transfer. Mum travelled to the bush all the time for her work, but Dad never went along. Even I tagged along sometimes because it was fun to visit for a few days. But I couldn't imagine this being my home. Dad could've said no, but he was a consultant and could work from anywhere; he only needed his laptop and an Internet connection.

The drive to camp was long and bumpy, and my phone died, so I couldn't even listen to music. Peter went on and on about how much we'd love it there. At least the air conditioning worked. The cool air was nice as I stared out the window and drowned out Peter's voice. I had a knack for blocking out people's voices by placing my concentration elsewhere, an idiosyncrasy my mum didn't like about me. But she did the same thing—go figure!

She called me her idiosyncratic child because of my many quirky habits. My mum loved using words I didn't understand. She said she did it to help me develop a rich vocabulary. Whenever I didn't understand a word, she asked me to look it up in the dictionary. But when she wasn't listening, my dad whispered to me, 'That's rich coming from my idiosyncratic wife.' He lightened the mood when my mum and I got into it; our inside joke always made me laugh.

It was so green and thick, and everything looked hazy because of the *insane* heat. The drive through Mfuwe town was very different from a typical drive in our Lusaka neighbourhood. I thought of the huge Jacaranda trees along one side of Sable Road near our house in Kabulonga; purple flowers covered their branches that hung all the way over to the other side of the road, forming a huge arch. Kai and I rode our bikes down there a gazillion times a day and joked how our natural purple umbrellas provided shade from the hot sun. On the road, the fallen flowers formed a *royal purple carpet*. One time, we picked some flowers, and my dad had a go at us because bees rely on those Jacaranda flowers for food. We only stopped picking them because we didn't want the bees to sting us. As far as we saw, there were enough flowers to share with the bees. When the massive flamboyant tree by the driveway near our house dropped flowers, Kai joked it rolled out a red carpet, ready to welcome Her Royal Highness, Princess Kay home.

But here, I didn't see any Jacaranda or Flamboyant trees, only palm trees—everywhere. Peter said they are Vegetable Ivory Palms or Lala Palms—the palm leaves are green at the bottom and dry and yellow at the tips. It's the dry season, so the leaves are yellow. When I saw the first shop on the left, Captain Biggie General Dealers, it reminded me of a road trip when Kai and I listed all the strangely named shops and buildings. So, I decided to make a list of all the strange names here for Kai.

Next, I saw Uncle Petty Wholesale & Retail. Where did these names come from? Like, was 'Petty' the uncle's name, or was he a *petty person*? Then, there was People's Choice. I could almost hear Kai's voice ask: *Do you think we should give them an award?* Next, I saw Put God First Aunt Bwalya Hair Salon, and next door was the Three Hebrews Hair Salon. Kai would've had a field day with that name—'Maybe aunt Bwalya was a nun, woken up in the middle of the night by a voice or vision that said, "Put God first in all you do," and aunt Bwalya's response was probably, *"Saht eksay, not what you're tuning Bally"[4]* but when she opened her hair salon, the voice still rang in her head, so she decided to add "put God first." I wondered if they were really Hebrews or if someone decided to take the three wise men from the Bible and name a hair salon after them?'

Next, I saw All for All Shopping Centre, a small red building with white lettering. It didn't look like much of a shopping centre when I compared it to Pick n Pay or Shoprite in Lusaka. I tried to think of something clever about All for All. Then, I saw Just Africa Shop. Who knows what they sold in there? The name sounded like a craft shop, but it didn't look like it from the outside.

My mum got excited when she saw Tribal Textiles Shop & Café. 'What do you say we have our tea dates here, Bug?' she asked.

I kept my gaze out the window and pretended I hadn't heard her. Then, I saw a sign for Malimba Primary School. It looked nothing like my old school. Wow, it felt strange saying *my old school*. Maybe I could go to this school instead of doing online classes. Before we left home, we started online classes because too many people fell ill and needed to learn from home.

Next, I saw Step By Step, a tiny shop no bigger than the guest loo at our house in Kabulonga. It made me laugh when I imagined Kai saying something like, *Step by Step? It's more like Teeny Tiny Steps; your treehouse is bigger than that shop!*

Quite a few stalls with reed mats lined the roadside along with some small pan brick buildings and grass-thatched stores. Next to a small stand-alone building called Boxer Customer Shopping Centre was a little green shop called Cool Runnings. I watched the movie *Cool Runnings* with my dad to humour him; he got so excited when it came on DSTV. I wanted to point the store out to him but remembered I wasn't talking to any of them. So, instead, I carried on my gaze out the window. Suddenly, I would have given anything to go on one of those supermarket runs with my mum. I always complained about going with her, but I didn't see a single Shoprite, Spar, or Pick n Pay here. Did the Cool Runnings store stock my favourite cereal? Will I find Salt n Vinegar Pringles in All for All Shopping Centre? I thought about all the boxes of different teas my mum packed; she drank all sorts of hot teas and didn't care if it was 100 degrees outside! But she didn't give us a heads up to bring our favourite goodies. Ughhhh, I hate it here!

The moment I said a little prayer for God to take me away from here, I saw a Mosque and a Jehovah's Witness church. Hopefully, that'd be a sign for a quickly answered prayer.

The sign for the Women's Bike Association made sense; I saw more bicycles than cars on the road, and loads of women rode their bikes with babies *papad* (babies placed on their mothers' backs in a cloth sling called a chitenge). Some of the babies had their heads tucked under the chitenges, and others popped their heads out like little meerkats, trying to look ahead. Some kids rode bikes three times their size. I imitated my mum, saying, 'They'll grow into them' because she always bought us clothes three times our size and said we'd grow into them.

Some people rode bikes with piles of firewood stacked at the rear; others had three crates of beer and egg trays piled one on top of the other *while* talking on their mobile phones. Women walked with baskets and other goods stacked on their heads. Further ahead, I saw stalls with second-hand clothes and others with fruits and vegetables. My aunt liked to call the stalls 'Sallies,' but their real name was Salaula.

As we left town and approached the game park, the road got bumpier with more gravel and many camp signs. The Flatdogs Camp caught my eye; I wondered what kind of camp that was. Peter saw the puzzled look on my face through the rear-view mirror.

'A flat dog is what the Australians call a crocodile. There are quite a number of crocodiles in the river, so it's a clever name for the camp.' I nodded to him in the mirror, and he smiled back.

As we crossed the bridge and approached the checkpoint into the South Luangwa National Park, a tower of giraffes stood a few metres from the road reserve. First, I wondered if my eyes were playing tricks on me because they appeared out of nowhere. Giraffes were my absolute favourite animals, so tall, so regal, so elegant. My mum gave me a stuffed hand-me-down giraffe when I was a baby, originally from her dad when she was born. She never gave him a name, so I named him Mwana (which means baby, but it could also mean friend depending on the pronunciation). My mum said I clutched onto him tightly and never let go. 'Look at that, Bug, your faves have come to welcome you,' my mother said. I ignored her and acted like I wasn't interested. There was no way I'd let them think I was okay with any of this.

It was pretty cool to see the giraffes first. I was—*am*—obsessed with them. The giraffe family gave me a warm fuzzy feeling, and I squeezed Mwana tightly. It's difficult to explain, but for the first time, I felt like I had some connection with Shikulu. My phone was dead, or I would have used Snapchat to contact Kai to show him the cool giraffe. I missed Kai so much. We would have laughed if we were together. Kai—his real name was Sekai—was my next-door neighbour. We grew up in each other's homes, went to school together, and spent weekends and holidays together. It felt weird not seeing him every day. I teared up at that thought.

My Jack Russel, Zozo, always sensed when I was sad and did some silly trick to cheer me. I missed him too! He stayed with Mbuya, who pretended she didn't like him because he chewed her doormats and dug in her garden, but many times, she laughed when he did silly things like chase after butterflies. I wondered what he was doing now—probably driving Mbuya crazy. Oh, how I already missed my visits with Mbuya. I should've fought harder to stay with her, but Mum convinced me when she said, 'Who's going to take my side when the boys gang up on me?' I fell for that line all the time.

We waited in the minivan as Peter went to the checkpoint for paperwork. He left the car and aircon running. A man walked by carrying fish on what looked like a string or a line of some sort. Mwezi was still excited about the giraffe and talked about all the other animals he couldn't wait to see. He rambled on about dinosaurs and asked my dad if there were any in the bush. Finally, Peter returned to the car, and we drove off.

More sadness grew inside of me. Mbuya always used some saying or proverb as an answer to life's problems. She'd say, '*Kasuba, limbula sansa tailatwala mishila.*' The direct translation was 'uproot a tree before it spreads its roots.' But the true message was 'nip it in the bud.' She always gave me a literal translation, but the actual point still went over my head.

I continued to gaze out the window as we left the security checkpoint and crossed the Luangwa bridge. Flat dogs (crocodiles) sunbathed on the riverbank. Further down, I saw a fisherman on his canoe, waiting for his catch. He looked like he was standing on a tight rope, trying to keep his balance. The man at the checkpoint must've bought the fish from him. On the other side of the river, a large pod of hippos wallowed in the river below the bridge. There were so many of them with their heads buoyed slightly above the water, their eyes peeked, and tiny ears pointed upwards; some of them made honking sounds. They resembled rocks floating in the water. It reminded me of bobbing for apples.

I chuckled to myself as I recalled Kai's voice saying, *Imagine Ms. Chibanda bobbing for hippos.* She was our grade teacher, but Chibanda (ghost) wasn't her real name. Kai gave her the name when she introduced us to Halloween and the game called 'bobbing for apples.' She was new at our school, a Muzungu (white) American woman very excited about getting our class into the Halloween spirit. Of course, we all knew about Halloween from television, but we weren't too interested because everyone found the whole Halloween concept strange. We didn't understand why anyone dressed as ghosts, bobbed for apples, and knocked on strangers' doors asking for sweets. Kai joked about her being a ghost because she was obsessed with Halloween, and the name stuck.

The other animals along the way excited me. The hippos felt so close yet so far. It all seemed so surreal and a little crazy. Hours ago, I watched *Madagascar* on TV, and there in front of me was the real Gloria with her extended family!

Nothing could have prepared me for what happened next. As we approached the entrance of the lodge, two massive lions sat on the roadside.

'Oh, look, Garlic and Ginger are here to welcome us,' Peter said.

'Oh, wow! Pet lions! I can't wait to play with them,' Mwezi exclaimed.

'No, no, my friend. As lions go, these two are on the friendly side, but they are still wild animals. They like laying around here from time to time—but remember, they're dangerous. You must never approach them or any other animal for that matter,' Peter said.

'Do they come into the lodge?' I asked.

'No, no. Sometimes, we do get visits from elephants. They like to eat the mangoes, and the Vervet monkeys always hang around. But stay out of their way, and they'll keep away from you—you must never feed them!' Peter responded.

It scared me when I saw the lions and when Peter talked about animals entering the lodge. Mwezi, on the other hand, was excited at the thought of all these animals roaming around freely at our new home. *Our new home?* I still couldn't believe it—stuck here with nothing but my annoying little brother and a troop of monkeys for company.

REFLECTION

Here are Kasuba's questions at the beginning of the story.
Do you ever feel like everyone apart from you has a say in what happens in your life? Your mum, your dad, your teachers? Do you ever feel powerless, like you just have to go with the flow and whatever you want doesn't matter?
Have you ever been in a situation where you felt like you had no power over a decision that would affect your life?
How did you feel?
Do you identify with what Kasuba's going through?
Remember, there's no right or wrong answer. This page has been deliberately left blank for you to fill in your answers.

PART 2
RESISTANCE

Resistance *noun*

dislike of or opposition to a plan, an idea, etc.; the
act of refusing to obey[5]

CHAPTER 2
I DON'T WANT TO BE HERE

As I stepped out of the minivan and headed towards the main building entrance, the peacefulness of the whole place amazed me. The calm drew me in—I'd never felt that anywhere else—I thought I would have to try hard to like this place. *Why did I even think like that?* It certainly wasn't the plan. The bush and travelling must have messed with my mind.

'Where can I charge my phone?' I asked Peter.

'Bug, settle in first. You haven't even seen your room yet, and you're already thinking about your phone,' my mother said.

I didn't even bother responding. What would be the point? No one cared what I thought anyway.

Peter looked at me with sympathetic eyes. 'Come on, give me your phone. I'll plug it in, so it'll charge while you look around. You won't get a great signal in your room anyway. Go to the library for the best signal, and there's WIFI there too.'

I didn't find anything funny about that, but it made my mum and dad chuckle.

My first night was awful; I cried myself to sleep. The only person I wanted to speak with was Kai, but I couldn't find a spot with a great phone signal. My parents lied to me! They told me everyone was only a phone call away. How could I speak to anyone without a signal? Everyone got up before 5:00 a.m.

19

to go on a stupid game drive. Not only did my parents drag me into the middle of nowhere, they expected me to be up at *stupid o'clock* to look at stupid animals! Unfortunately, I woke up anyway because of the ngoma (drum) alarm. How was it someone's sole purpose to get up before 5:00 a.m. every day to beat a drum to wake everyone to look at animals? Isn't that what the National Geographic Channel was for?

Since I was up and my parents weren't there to bother me, I thought I'd check the place out before they got back. My mum was a stickler for schedules; we could do online school in our own time, but she had a plan all laid out for Mwezi and me. My online school would be in the library until I started boarding school in South Africa next term. I honestly didn't want to go to boarding school when my parents first suggested it. They both went to boarding schools in England, and my mum said she had some of the best years of her life there. I didn't believe her and thought it was her way of convincing me to go. She said she chose the school in South Africa because it was easy to visit me and reminded her of her boarding school in Canterbury, England. Suddenly, I looked forward to boarding school. I bet they had good WIFI there, and anywhere else had to be better than this place.

I finally found the library. Peter was right; the signal there *was* really great. Finally, I could speak to Kai. He wouldn't be up yet but wouldn't mind me calling him this early.

'Hey, sleepyhead, wake up!'

'Kay! It's you!' Kai sounded pleased to hear my voice.

'Well, who else would be calling you this early? Like, how many people do you know who live in the bush? I'm telling you, Kai, this place is crazy, and the people here are nuts. Everyone gets up before sunrise,' I said all in one breath.

'Kay, tell me everything!' Kai sounded excited.

The only thing I was excited about was finally talking to my bestie. 'There's not a lot to tell. I wish you were here. Kai, I hate this place. At least if you were here, we'd start our own little adventure! It would be epic!' I said.

'Come on, Kay. It can't be that bad. Give it a chance,' Kai said.

'You're right, Kai.' I rolled my eyes.

'What has the bush done to you? You're admitting I'm right!' Kai sounded genuinely surprised. Maybe it was still too early in the day for his brain to process the sarcastic tone in my voice.

'Sure, Kai. It's not that bad. This place makes Mrs Chibanda's maths challenges look like fun, so it's not that bad—it's worse!' I said.

'The *perf*[6] *queen*! I thought the bush would have tamed you. One night there and your drama levels have skyrocketed!' Kai responded.

'Kai, it really is *that bad*. Every morning at *stupid o'clock*, someone beats an actual drum to wake us up. Oh, and I'm not talking percussion, but these are real ngomas in the village they beat at your cousin's Matebeto (a traditional ceremony which is part of the marriage rites). They go on and on until we're all up,' I said.

'*Mmmmmm, saht eksay.*[7] There's no way it's as bad as that *ohn*[8] who cycles past our road every morning with his megaphone, blaring *full blast,* trying to get people to sell their old car batteries and broken geysers to him,' Kai responded.

We both broke into a chorus of our best impression of the old battery-shopper's megaphone voice: '*Ma battery yo sila ya motoka na ma geyser yo sila tigulaaaaaaaaa!*' The translation was 'We buy old car batteries and broken geysers.' Then, we both laughed. It reminded me of how it was when we walked to school together. Stories never ended as long as the two of us were together.

'See! You're laughing, so that's a good thing. You'll get used to it,' Kai said.

I wanted to tell him the only reason I laughed was because of him, but before I could say anything, he said, 'Listen, Kay, *I have to dip,*[9] you know how *the Bally*[10] gets when I'm late for school. Let's chat later. It'll get better; you'll see.' Then, the line cut.

Kai always had a way of cheering me up. As rushed as our phone call was, I smiled when I thought about how I hated the sound of that man's voice blaring from the megaphone. But now, I would give anything to be back home and hear it again. If I could go back home, I would never complain about that megaphone ever again.

My smile turned into a frown, and before I knew it, I sobbed and felt worse than I did before speaking with Kai. I hated it so much here; I wanted to go home!

REFLECTION

Have you ever been in a situation of change? A move to a new town or a new school? What feelings did you have? Can you identify with Kasuba's feelings and actions? What advice would you give her? This part has been deliberately left blank for you to write down your thoughts.

PART 3
REALISATION

Realisation *noun*

the process of becoming aware of something[11]

CHAPTER 3
I'M GOING TO BE HERE FOR A WHILE

I didn't even hear Peter approach because my thoughts circled my feelings. I heard Kai's voice singing in my head, *Kay-Kay, do you love me . . . are you riding* (to the tune of Drake's "In My Feelings"). It made me smile on the inside, but I was still really sad.

'Miss Kay, are you alright?' Peter asked.

I didn't respond to him and carried on sobbing. It was weird hearing him call me Miss Kay like I was some kind of lady, but I liked it; it made me seem important.

'Didn't you want to go on the game drive?' he asked.

I didn't respond.

'You know, this place isn't that bad. You need to give it a chance,' he said.

'What was that you said? The mantra of the morning? First, Kai, now you!' I said.

As soon as I said it, I knew it was rude, so I bit my lower lip and apologised.

Peter looked at me with pity. 'I know it doesn't seem like it now, but soon, you'll grow to love it here.' He persisted.

'Come with me. There's something I want to give to you,' he added.

I got up, and we walked to his office in silence. When we got there, I looked around and saw what looked like an ancient television with some weird box thing underneath it. 'What is that?' I asked, pointing at the box-shaped object underneath the TV.

'This is a VCR,' Peter said.

'What does it do? And why isn't your television flat? Is it even a television? Does it work?' I asked.

Peter laughed. 'Yes, it is a television, and it has served me well for many years. Your shikulu gave it to me.'

'Really? I guess that's cool; it's vintage,' I responded.

'Yes, vintage. I like that. He also gave me the VCR, and we used to watch training videos on Conservation Management and Human-Animal Conflict. Or, sometimes, we watched movies together. Your shikulu's favourite movie was *Coming to America*. He used to joke about how us young kids dreamt about going to America, but eventually, we realised we hold the true wealth right here at home.' He smiled.

All the stuff he said about America went right over my head. I went to New York with my mum when I was little. It was cold, and there was no yard for me to run around. She would have had to take me to a park, so I only wanted to come back home. 'How do you watch movies from that big box?' I asked, but before he answered, I said, 'Actually, don't worry; I'll Google™ it.'

Peter shook his head and shrugged. He pulled out a pamphlet from the top drawer of his desk and handed it to me. 'We usually share this with our young visitors. It's a game to make the stay more interesting. There's a list of some of the well-known species of animals in the Luangwa Valley. The aim is to tick off as many as you can each time you see and identify one. Oh, and you have to see them in real life, not on some Internet search with Google,' he explained.

'Internet search with Google,' I responded, trying to do my best impression of him. 'Wow, Mr P, who even says that?'

He laughed and said, 'Look at you, giving me a nickname. Mr P, I like it.'

'What a long list,' I said, almost defeated as I looked at the pamphlet.

'Well, if you had gone on the game drive, you would have already started ticking quite a few of them off,' he said in his know-it-all voice.

'Has anyone ever identified all the animals on the list?' I asked.

'Well, let's put it this way. I've lived here most of my life, and I have seen maybe sixty percent of the animals on that list,' he responded.

'What's the point of the game then?' I asked.

'Well, right now, a young boy from America holds the record. He managed to identify over forty species in the week he and his family came on safari here. Do you think you can do better?'

I never backed down from a challenge, and if some American kid could identify forty species in a week, I was determined to get to eighty in half the time. 'Sure! I can easily beat that,' I said.

'So, I see you're competitive, just like your shikulu,' Peter responded with a smile.

I liked it when he mentioned my grandpa.

Looking up from the paper, I asked, 'Can you tell me about my shikulu?'

Peter paused and then said, 'He was a good man and great with the animals. I have many stories about him, but I have to get to work now. There's plenty of time for us to catch up later, and you should start on the list if you want to beat that record! Close the door behind you when you leave the office,' he said as he walked out of the office.

I took a closer look at the list. It was very long; there were over 400 bird species alone. Then, it hit me—I was going to be there for a long, long time!

In the middle of the list was a picture of a very colourful bird. It looked like a parrot, but it had a different name, Lillian's Lovebird. I guess it was a kind of parrot. As I looked up from the pamphlet, the same bird perched on the edge of Peter's office window. I wasn't sure if it was there or if my mind played tricks on me. But it sure looked real with its orange head, red-tipped beak, and white rings around its red-brown eyes. It had a permanently surprised look on its face. I never noticed when I first looked at the picture on the pamphlet, but it didn't have a nose.

'Do birds have noses?' I asked myself out loud.

'Can't you tell the difference between a nose and a beak?' the bird responded.

It startled me. 'Wait. Am I seeing and hearing things? Did you just speak?'

'You're not exactly the sharpest tool in the box, are you?' the bird responded.

I was freaking out. *Did this bird actually talk to me?* 'I mean, I know parrots can talk, but they only repeat stuff, right?' I spoke out loud again.

'Right,' the bird said.

'Mwezi, is that you?' Maybe my brother was playing tricks on me.

'No, but if you want to be on a first-name basis, you can call me Kuseniseni. Do you have any food around here a guy could eat?' the bird responded.

'OMG! You really *are* talking!' I whispered in a state of disbelief.

'Nothing gets past you! And why are you doing that?' the bird asked.

I pinched myself to make sure I wasn't dreaming. 'Kai would never believe this! So, Lillian's Lovebirds can *actually* talk?' I said to try and convince myself more than anything else.

'We prefer to be called Nyasa birds and please, less of the love for me. I'm more of a fighter than a lover,' Kuseniseni responded.

I chuckled. 'Sure, you are. So, Kuseniseni, as in . . .'

Before I could finish, the bird said, 'Don't even think about making jokes about early birds. Besides, we don't even eat worms.'

'Oh,' I responded.

I didn't notice, but at some point, Peter came back to the office. 'Miss Kay, you're still here? Who are you talking to?' he asked.

'Ummmm, the bird on the windowsill.' I looked at him like his question had the most obvious answer.

'Oh, really?' he said and looked towards the window. 'Ahhh, a Nyasa! Did you tick him off your list?' he said, glancing toward the window.

Before I had a chance to respond, he carried on, 'You're quite lucky to see one. There've been several cases of poisoning lately. Farmers don't like them because they eat their millet and seeds.'

'So, they poisoned them? That's mean; can't they just chase them away?' Before Peter responded, I added, 'Well, Kuseniseni mentioned he was hungry.'

'Kuseniseni?' Peter asked.

'The bird,' I responded. *Like obviously.*

'And he told you he was hungry?' he asked, and I realised how silly I sounded.

'Gosh, this guy is even quicker off the mark than you are!' Kuseniseni said in a mocking voice.

I chuckled again, then said to Peter, 'Yeah, didn't you hear him just now?'

'Remember what I told you the day you arrived? We don't feed the animals here. Not even cute little Nyasa birds that tell you they are hungry.' Peter chuckled.

I could tell he was teasing me, but I didn't say anything. Maybe this was *The Secret Life of Pets* situation, where I was the only one who could hear the bird talk.

He glanced out the window and continued, 'Well, I only came to pick up my notepad. Everyone got back from the game drive. You need to go and join them for breakfast before your first day of online school. And I can see why you named him Kusenseni. He's an early bird, but he won't be catching any worms. He's not the worm-eating type!'

I gave Peter a dry smile.

As he walked out of the office, he said, 'You know, your shikulu used to joke about talking to animals as well. You are just like him. Anyway, as cute as Kuseniseni is, please do not feed him.'

'Are you going to listen to that guy? So, you get to have breakfast, and I get nothing! You know, we eat the farmers' seeds because they cut down all our trees and burn them,' Kuseniseni said.

'That's terrible! Why would they do that?' I asked.

'You should know—you're one of them. Humans do nutty stuff!' Kuseniseni said.

'We really do,' I responded.

I turned to Kuseniseni and asked, 'Well, what do you usually eat?'

'Fruit and seeds and stuff, but you heard the guy. The farmers are poisoning their seeds and leaving them out there to bait us. It's not just them; the poachers are doing it too!' he lamented.

'That's awful. Okay. See that thatched building over there? My room is on the other side. Go and wait by the window, and I'll grab something for you at breakfast,' I said.

Kuseniseni flew off the windowsill, and I dashed to the restaurant where my family already sat at the table.

Mum yelled at me before I even got to the table, 'Kay! Why are you still in your pyjamas? School starts in less than thirty minutes, and I expect you to be on time.'

'Sorry, Mum, I started exploring and got carried away. I'll take some fruit and go get ready!'

Normally, Mum would have made me sit at the table, but I never ate fruit. When she heard me say I'd grab fruit, all her Christmases and birthdays must have arrived at once. Me eating fruit was a *big* deal for her.

I grabbed some lychees, a couple of bananas, a mango, and dashed to my room. A part of me expected not to find Kuseniseni waiting for me on the windowsill—like I imagined the whole thing. I wanted him to be there, but he wasn't by the window and not anywhere else when I looked around when I got there.

'Did I just make it all up? Maybe because I didn't sleep much last night, I imagined the whole thing.'

'Imagined what? You know, you really shouldn't leave your window open without the mosquito netting shutters. Anything could get in. Oh, and do you always talk to yourself?' Kuseniseni said.

Kuseniseni was perched on the top of the bookshelf next to my bed. I was so happy to see him since I had begun to question my sanity. Walking over to the bookshelf, I put the fruit next to him. 'I didn't know what you liked, so I grabbed a bunch of different things.'

'Fruit is fruit. Oh, lychees! Jackpot! You did good, girl.' Kuseniseni pecked at that lychee, removed the hard, outer skin layer, and ate the flesh and seeds in no time.

I was really impressed and said, 'Wow! You can do a lot with that beak, huh?'

Kuseniseni didn't respond as he devoured the lychee.

'Listen, I need to get ready for school,' I said to him.

'Don't you mean online school? How does that work?' he asked.

'Well, basically, all my lessons come on this tablet. It's like being in class, but this tablet represents the teacher and the board. This will be my life until I go to boarding school at the beginning of next year,' I responded as I picked up my iPad.

'That sounds complicated. Don't worry about me, kid; you go ahead. Hey, let's do breakfast again tomorrow, but slightly earlier, as my name suggests. I'm an eat at the crack of dawn kind of guy. I'll be here before the ngoma beats.'

'Wow! That early? Sure, Kuseniseni, see you tomorrow.' I didn't mind what time he came; this was the most exciting thing that's happened to me in like, forever.

Funny, I thought it would be a long three months, but things started to get interesting.

REFLECTION

Change is a funny thing. Some people jump up, excited about change. They take it on as one big adventure. Others are more cautious and have a wait-and-see attitude. Then, there are those who don't like change at all; they don't even want to give it a chance. What they don't understand is change helps us stretch out of our comfort zone; it helps us to grow and see things from a new perspective. Change is the only constant in life, which is a bit of an oxymoron, but it's true. Think about how you deal with change. Are you like Kasuba, who thinks she doesn't want the change but bit by bit gives it a chance? Or are you somewhere else along the change spectrum? This part has been deliberately left blank for you to write down your thoughts.

PART 4

REASSESSMENT

Reassessment *noun*

the act of thinking again about something to decide
if you need to change your opinion of it[12]

CHAPTER 4
WHAT ARE MY OPTIONS?

I woke up to a pecking sound on my window. What time was it? It must have been early—I hadn't heard the beat of the ngomas yet. When I opened the blinds, Kuseniseni was on the other side of the window, and he stared at me with his wide, white-ringed reddish-brown eyes. He flew in when I opened the window, spotted the guava on my dresser, and pecked away at it.

'Sorry, there was no fruit at dinner, so I snuck it out of Peter's office. I hope he doesn't notice. When you said you're an early eater, I didn't seriously think you meant before the sun was up. Enjoy your guava; I'm going back to bed,' I said and threw the sheet over my head.

'Not a morning person, huh! I guess I'll go and tell the rest of the gang you're not interested in meeting them,' Kuseniseni said.

'Rest of the gang?' I asked. 'Who are you talking about?'

'You know, everyone else who lives around here. I told them all about you, and they're really excited about meeting you, but I guess I'll have to tell them it was too early for *Princess Kay*,' he responded.

'Hold on, do you mean like other Nyasa birds? Do they also talk like you?' My curiosity piqued.

'Yeah, Nyasas and a few other species,' he responded.

If he had eyebrows, I'm sure he would have raised them. 'There are other birds who talk?' I was super excited.

'Look, just come with me, and you'll see for yourself,' he said as he flew out the open window.

More talking birds? I tried to wrap my head around Kuseniseni, but my curiosity got the better of me. I thought of Kai and how he wouldn't even think twice about this. I heard his voice in my head. *What are you waiting for, Kay? It's talking birds; go already!*

'Okay, fine! Let me get out of my pyjamas and put some-thing else on,' I said to Kuseniseni, who had flown back and perched himself on the windowsill.

I quickly put on some sweatpants and a hoodie and slid my feet into my Crocs™.

Kuseniseni took one look at them and said, 'Whoa! What are those? I thought you'd be going for a look to make a good first impression!'

'*Ahhh. Iwe naiwe*'[13] (pronounced ee-way nah ee-way) I said. 'Crocs are comfy. Besides, I need to get back before anyone notices I'm gone, so there's no time for the fashion police, hosted by Kuseniseni!'

I slid the mosquito screen fully open and positioned myself to jump off the windowsill but heard the beating sound of the ngomas. It startled me, and I lost my balance and fell off the ledge and grazed my elbow on the grass. I brushed it off and quickly followed Kuseniseni, who had already flown ahead. We went along the edge of the dry riverbed, and when out of sight from the lodge, Kuseniseni stopped and said, 'I'm guessing the K in Miss Kay doesn't stand for *Kim Possible*? What was that? Were you trying to get us caught?'

'Ha! Ha! Very funny! The drums startled me, that's all. So, I slipped.'

'Sure!' Kuseniseni responded. 'That ngoma beat happens at the same time every morning from Sunday to Sunday; it's not like it was a surprise!'

'Well, it's only my second day here. I'm still not used to it,' I responded.

'Okay. How am I going to introduce you to the gang? Miss Kay? Or is it Princess Kay?' Kuseniseni asked.

I paused for a second, and Kuseniseni said, 'What's the matter, Princess, already tired?'

'No, it's just that Kai calls me Princess, and I wondered what it would be like if he was here with us.'

'Who's Kai?' Kuseniseni asked.

'My best friend. He's in Lusaka; you kinda remind me of him,' I said in an emotional, nostalgic voice.

'Well, don't get any ideas, Princess; I'm nobody's BFF,' he said matter of factly.

'Really? I find that hard to believe.' I laughed.

'Alright, Princess. Sarcasm does not look good on you!'

'Enough with calling me *Princess*! My name is actually Kasuba, but everyone calls me Kay.' Him calling me Princess really made me miss Kai.

'Kasuba, like the sun. Regular ray of sunshine you are!' he said.

'Oh! Now who's being sarcastic?' I responded.

As I said that, the sun peeked out, such an amazing sight. I watched the sunrise, caught up in the moment and didn't notice the other animals gather around the waterhole.

'You get to see this every day,' I said to Kuseniseni, but he wasn't there; he'd flown ahead to the other animals.

'Good Morning, your Majesty,' I heard a voice say.

When I turned around and saw a wildebeest do what looked like a curtsey, I screamed and ran off in the direction of the lodge. Suddenly, Kuseniseni appeared ahead of me, and I stopped.

'Relax, Princess. Munyu won't hurt you.'

The wildebeest approached again. He did a half curtsey while walking—if I wasn't so frightened, I would have laughed. 'I'm sorry, your royal highness, I didn't mean to scare you,' he said.

On top of the fear, I tried to wrap my head around a curtseying, talking wildebeest.

'Your royal highness? I said she *behaves* like a Princess; I didn't say she's real-life royalty.' Kuseniseni scoffed mid-laughter.

I took a deep breath and a closer look at Munyu. The wildebeest spoke to me, and I tried to make sense of it all. Kuseniseni was a kind of parrot, so in my head, it made sense he could talk. Like, he was an *advanced* parrot, but a talking wildebeest? What logical explanation was there?

'Are you going to react like this each time you meet one of the gang? They're really excited about meeting you, but now I think I hyped you up a little too much.' Kuseniseni's voice faded as the animals from the waterhole walked towards us, and all seemed to talk simultaneously. Maybe I was still dreaming, and the excitement of yesterday's activities had my imagination running wild. I pinched myself to wake up, but that didn't work, so I slapped myself twice on both cheeks. When that didn't work either, the animals stared at me.

'What's wrong with her?' the giraffe asked.

'Oh, she did the pinching thing when she first met me! But the slapping thing? That's new,' Kuseniseni said.

'Don't worry. I completely understand because I also have a few medical conditions. Like, my heavy head and oh, my heart is really big. My blood pressure is always through the roof, but that's probably because I only sleep four hours in a day—the secret is to keep active. You see, that's how I keep the blood pressure at bay, and I've been carrying this child in my belly for the last fourteen and a half months. But I don't beat myself up over it,' the giraffe said and looked at me with empathy in her eyes.

If I were a fainter, that would've been when it would have happened. Instead, I only stood there. *Forget the wildebeest. Did that giraffe not only talk to me but give a run-down of her medical history and implied I also have some medical condition?* I started to feel a little lightheaded. My all-time favourite animal talked to me, but I couldn't find any words to respond.

'Alright, Ms Lulumba, that's enough,' a really mature and wise sounding voice said. 'Can't you see the poor child is overwhelmed?'

I saw an owl perched on a powdery brown branch in the Ivungula (sausage tree). 'Pululu (pronounce poo-loo-loo) is right. I didn't think this whole introduction thing through.' Before Kuseniseni could finish, a little voice came from behind a mama elephant.

'Mummy, please let me see the Princess.' The mama elephant stepped aside, and the cutest little baby elephant appeared with the biggest smile on his face. As he walked towards me, he tripped over his trunk, got up, and tripped again.

It was such a funny sight, but he seemed so determined to walk properly, so I didn't laugh. Finally, I found my voice. 'Hi there,' I said in the same cooing voice adults use when speaking to babies. When I took a step towards him, mama elephant put her body in between us. It caught me by surprise and scared me so much; I tripped and fell.

'Oh, come on, Mama Njovu. Stop flexing your muscles. You know the girl means no harm,' Pululu said.

I got up and apologised.

Mama Njovu turned around and swished her tail from side to side. The tail hair caught the tip of my nose. 'I know. I don't want her getting too familiar,' she said as she sashayed her way back to the watering hole. The baby elephant followed behind and carried on, tripping over his trunk. I watched him as he reached for Mama Njovu's breast while she still walked. He went underneath her, trying to suckle and walk at the same time. It was one of the funniest and most bizarre things I'd ever seen. Well, apart from all the talking animals, of course.

Mama Njovu wallowed in the water. The poor baby elephant stuck his trunk in his mouth and started to suck on it, maybe for comfort in the same way human babies suck their thumbs or pacifiers.

'That's strange. I never realised elephant calves suckled with their mouths. I always thought they used their trunks,' I said.

'Kay, didn't you see how many times that child tripped over his trunk? He had no idea what to do with that thing!' Kuseniseni said.

'He doesn't know yet, but he'll learn when the time is right,' Pululu said.

'I wish I could stay here all day, but I need to get back in time for breakfast before my parents send out a search party for me. It was nice meeting you all. I promise not to freak out the next time I see you,' I said.

There was a chorus of laughter from the different animals by the watering hole. As I skipped back to the lodge, I felt different, excited about being here. There was a shift in my whole demeanour; I couldn't wait to see what happened tomorrow.

The whole day, I thought about my new friends and could hardly concentrate on my lessons. My mum monitored our online classes and was so irritated with my absent-mindedness; she dismissed class early. At lunch, I continued to daydream about the morning's events. Peter asked me a question, but I didn't even hear him. I didn't even realise he had joined us for lunch.

'Miss Kay, are you alright?'

'Good luck getting anything out of this one today. She's been stuck in her own world since morning,' my mum replied on my behalf.

'How's your list coming along? Have you spotted any more animals?' he asked me.

'Oh, yes, I have. 'I take it with me everywhere, just in case I spotted something,' I finally replied as I pulled the pamphlet out of my back pocket and handed it over to him.

Peter browsed through the list and looked at me. Then, he looked back at the list. 'I see you've been quite busy!'

'Yes,' I responded and then paused, thinking of what to say next. 'I got up early this morning to get a WIFI signal from the library. Then, I saw all these animals gathered by the waterhole. There's a great view from the deck outside the library. I saw so many different animals gathered around to drink.'

'That was very early; you must've caught them as the sun came up. But the watering hole is still quite far off to see with the naked eye.'

'Umm, yeah, I did. It was cool. I, um, borrowed Dad's binoculars and got a great view.'

'I was wondering where those were!' my dad said, looking up from his plate.

'Yeah, sorry I didn't ask, Dad.'

He smiled at me and carried on eating his meal.

'I see you even gave the animals names,' Mr P added.

When I got back from the waterhole, I had checked off all the animals I saw and wrote their names down to call each one by name the next time I saw them. As Mr P mentioned me naming them, I tried to recall them in the order I met them. So, there was Munyu, the wildebeest; Ms Lulumba, the giraffe; Pululu, the owl; Mama Njovu; Sofu, the baby elephant; Munji, the warthog; Fubu, the hippopotamus; Mpala, the impala; Nja, the red lechwe; Nkhamba Nkhamba—Egyptian geese (because they always talked); Chimbwi, the hyena; Chuzu, the Waterbuck; and Kopekope, the red billed hornbill. Mbwili, the leopard, was super unfriendly. Then, there was Kalamo, the king lion, and Naitwika, the queen lioness.

Pembele (Pem-bay-lay), the rhinoceros, didn't like me very much; okay, she didn't like me at all. Kuseniseni said he would explain, but we got distracted.

'Miss Kay, are you daydreaming again? I said you gave the animals names,' Mr P repeated himself.

'Ummm, yes. I thought it would be more fun if I gave them all a character,' I responded.

'Interesting, like the way you named the Nyasa bird, *Kuseniseni,*' he said as he carried on looking at the pamphlet.

'Yeah, exactly like that!' I responded, smiling.

'I'm glad you're enjoying the challenge, but I also see you gave the name to a rhino,' he said as he handed me back the pamphlet. I paused for a moment and recalled Pululu's words about Pembele: *Don't tell anyone about seeing Pembele. She's one of the last of her kind, and if poachers find out she's here, they'll come for her. Can we trust you to keep this to yourself?* I told her she could trust me.

I finally responded to Mr P, 'Yeah, I did it because I've always wanted to see a rhino. You've seen I didn't tick it off the list, though.'

He hesitated for a moment, then nodded and started to walk towards his office.

'Mr P! What happened to all the rhinos?' I called after him.

'Bug, I'm sure Peter has a lot to do. Stop bothering the man,' my mum said.

'Oh, no, Lutanda, I don't mind at all. This place was filled with so many black rhinos not so many years ago, but poachers were very ruthless, and we didn't have the kind of patrols and support we have now. They eventually cleared them until they were extinct in this area. As you know, your shikulu fought hard to try and protect them. They became extinct in Zambia over twenty years ago.' His eyes lit up whenever he talked about my shikulu.

'Around about the time that shikulu died?' I asked.

'Yes. He died saving the last black rhino we knew of,' Mr P responded.

'Why do you say *knew of*? Could there have been others you didn't see?' I asked.

'There were rumours she could've had the calf before the poachers killed her. She was pregnant, you see. But if she did, we would have found it. There's no way a calf could've survived out here without its mother.'

Now, it makes sense why Pemeble didn't like me. The poachers took her mum away from her when she was only a baby. She probably thought all people were the same.

Mr P looked at me and added, 'Don't look so sad. You know, up in the North Luangwa, they reintroduced black rhinos into the habitat. This time, they are very well protected. Perhaps one day, we can go up there, and you can see your very first black rhino.'

'That would be amazing!' I responded, not sharing I already saw my very first black rhino.

'Mr P, why do people cut down and burn the trees where the animals live?' I asked.

'You have lots of questions today. Well, you see, people mainly burn the trees for firewood and charcoal. You're right. It's destroying the habitat where the animals live. That's why birds eat farmers' seeds, and the larger herbivores—like the elephants—raid peoples' gardens,' he responded.

'If the people know it's bad for the animals, why do they do it? Why won't they stop? Can't you *make* them stop? I thought that was your job?' I emotionally replied as I thought about my new friends, especially Kuseniseni.

'I see this is important to you. You really are just like your grandfather. I wish it were that simple and straight forward. We have started some education campaigns for the local people. They focus on how we can live in harmony with our surroundings, but it takes time. If you like and your parents say it's okay, perhaps you can come along and see our outreach programmes. There's one where we take people on game drives in the park so they can appreciate and understand the ecosystem the animals live in and how we all have to play our part.' He smiled.

'I would love to do that,' I responded.

My mum and dad both looked at me and gave each other a puzzled look. Then, they looked back at me and said *yes!* in unison. My mum then added, 'Bug, I've never seen you this interested in anything, since, well, never.'

I smiled and said, 'I guess things are different here. I'm different.'

REFLECTION

Have you ever thought you didn't want something and made it a point to tell everyone who would listen you didn't want it? Then, circumstances changed, and you realised perhaps the something you didn't want was what you really needed? What was it about the circumstances that made you change your mind? Or did your perspective shift for another reason? This part has been deliberately left blank for you to write down your thoughts.

PART 5

REDISCOVERY

Rediscovery *noun*

the act or process of finding again something that
had been forgotten or lost[14]

CHAPTER 5
LISTENING TO MY INNER VOICE

Each day, I made an early morning visit to the waterhole. The animals welcomed me—except for Pembele. Even Mama Njovu liked me now. Sofu almost walked properly without tripping over his trunk every five minutes. Ms Lulumba had her baby but still complained about her ailments. Baby giraffes were even cuter than baby elephants. Unlike Sofu, the baby giraffe walked and ran a day after birth and was more graceful about suckling from Ms Lulumba. Her name was Lupili because she was born at the bottom of a hill. Ms Lulumba stood up, and it was like Lupili flew out of her. She landed with a thud and walked within thirty minutes. I thought of Mwezi and how excited we were when he started crawling at seven months. By nine and a half months, he stood and took a few steps. Everyone went on and on about how advanced he was for his age. When Lupili ran around at only a few days old, Mwezi's achievement seemed average at best.

I learned so much about animals, how they lived in harmony with their surroundings, and how they dealt with change with the seasons' ebb and flow. In a way, there wasn't much of a difference between humans and animals, except humans took a lot longer to adapt than animals did. Plus, we always tried to change things by making them *better*.

The impala were always together, and there were always so many of them. They even had their babies together. Pululu called it synchronised breeding. They all give birth at the same time in the afternoon to reduce the risk of preying predators. Lions hunt mostly at night and rest during the day. I guess that's why Garlic and Ginger spent their late mornings and afternoons chilling by the road near the lodge entrance.

Pululu explained, 'The impala move in large numbers, because when hunted by predators like lions, they can run fast and split up, which confuses the lions. Predators like lions run fast and expend energy quickly. Prey—like the impala—have more endurance and can run for extended periods without getting tired.'

'Oh, I get it. So, the predators are like Usain Bolt because he runs super fast over short distances, and the prey are like Brigid Kosgei because she's a world record marathon runner,' I said.

Pululu ignored my observation and carried on, 'The thing is, people and lions and other predators like to hunt impala because there are so many of them. Even when the impalas split up, humans are bound to catch one, especially the younger ones, because they are slower. So, the impala is a quick and tasty meal for them. They are kind of like the fast-food of the Savannah.'

'Oh, like MacDonald's! Is that why they all have a big M stamped on their bottoms?' I chuckled.

Pululu didn't get the reference until I told her about a quick and tender fast food place, like the impala. The restaurant's name had a big M like the impala did on their bottoms. I learned about how the impala followed baboons around because baboons picked fruit from high up in the trees, but they always dropped them. So, the impala ate the fallen fruit from the ground.

It amazed me how the animals relied on one another, but they didn't expect any payments or favours for the things they did for each other. I thought about my older cousins. They always complained about how they did something for someone but never received a returned favour.

The animals also liked to have fun with humans. During the mango season, the elephants walked right through the lodge's reception area to get to the mango trees at the back. It scared the humans at first, but they soon learned the elephants weren't there to hurt them and only wanted the mangoes.

One evening, Mbwili (leopard) chased an impala right into the lodge's dining area as people sat to have their dinner. That terrified the guests, but Mwezi was especially scared. He thought of all the warnings Peter had given about the wild animals and how dangerous they were. But I wasn't scared at all; I even got my mobile phone out and videoed everything. When I showed the video to the animals at the waterhole, they laughed so hard. I was sure one of the rangers from the camp by the lodge would come over and find out who caused such a raucous.

As I climbed through the window into my room that morning, Mwezi waited for me. 'Aha! I knew you were up to something. Where were you? I'm telling Mummy!'

'Telling Mummy what? The wind blew my drawing out of the window, and I climbed out to look for it before it flew too far down into the bush. Then, I'd have to tell Mum the leopard ate it!' I responded.

'The leopard?' Mwezi asked with a puzzled look on his face. I saw he wasn't buying my story.

'Yeah, brave boy. The same leopard you were so afraid of at dinner last night,' I responded.

'I wasn't scared!' he screamed back.

'Oh, really? Let's just watch this video on my phone to see how *not scared* you were!' I said.

'You're such a meany! I hate you. I'm telling on you!' he said, screaming and yelling to Mum as he left my room.

Mum came into my room and scolded me for making my brother cry. Then, she asked, 'And where do you disappear to so early in the morning? Mwezi said he can never find you.'

'That's coz I go to the library to get a signal on my phone, so I can message Kai,' I responded.

I felt bad about lying to my mother and Mwezi, and I felt awful about saying those horrid things to him and making him cry, but I couldn't risk him finding out about the animals.

The sound of Kuseniseni's beak pecking at my window every morning developed into a routine—He pecked, and I opened the window. He flew in and found the fruit on the top of my bookshelf, happily ate the fruit while I got dressed, then he flew out of the window. I climbed through and walked along the dry riverbed as he flew ahead. Today, though, something felt off. Before we arrived at the watering hole, I said to Kuseniseni, 'I think my brother grew suspicious about our morning meets. Suddenly, he grew interested in where I am every morning and asked why I wasn't scared when Mbwili did her little chase with the impala.'

'I thought you said he always has his head in the stars like his name—Mwezi,' Kuseniseni responded.

'He usually does—or it's stuck on his iPad—but now, he wants to know where I am every minute of the day. Maybe the bush got to him. I need to be more careful. Once he finds out, he'll definitely tell my parents. Then, it'll be bye-bye meetups,' Kuseniseni interrupted me before I could say more.

'Well, it's too late for that, Princess. He's behind those bushes!'

'Wait! What? Noooooo! I'm going to be in big trouble,' I said, really disappointed I hadn't noticed he had followed us.

'Hey, do you want me to scare the kid a little? You know, so he keeps his mouth shut?' Kuseniseni asked with a cold, evil grin.

'No, I'll talk to him.' So, I shouted to Mwezi, 'Hey, Bug-a-boo, I know you're behind that bush; you can come out now!'

'Are you crazy? Those animals will eat me! Actually, you *are* crazy! I heard you talking to that bird like it's a person,' Mwezi whispered.

'Wait, you heard Kuseniseni talk?' I said, surprised.

'Who is Kuseniseni?' Mwezi asked.

'The bird,' I responded, almost irritated.

'Oh, boy! Here we go again! So, this is the moon to your sun? Do your parents have a thing with objects in the sky?' Kuseniseni said.

I ignored Kuseniseni.

'No, I didn't hear the bird talk! You *really* are crazy. I'm telling Mum!' As Mwezi spoke, he saw the other animals walk towards us, and he screamed.

'Keep your voice down! It's alright,' I told him.

Then, he screamed even louder, but when he saw how calm I was, he asked, 'Wait, why aren't you scared? It's like at dinner the other night with the leopard. Remember what Peter said? "These are wild animals, and we shouldn't be anywhere near them." Seriously, they could eat us!' As the animals got closer, he screamed even louder.

'Shush, Mwezi! These are my friends; they won't hurt you,' I said.

'Your *friends*? Oh, wow. You are crazy!' Mwezi replied.

'No, Mwezi. Listen to me. You wanted to know what I did every morning? Well, this is it. I chill at the waterhole with my friends before the game drive so no one will see us.'

'Wow. You've lost it. These are not your *friends*. They are wild animals. We need to go before they eat us.' Mwezi was scared, and I needed to calm him down.

'If they were going to eat us, don't you think they would've done that by now? I know it's a lot to take in, but these *really are my friends*,' I said calmly.

'Your brother looks heated up there! I think Mama Njovu should squirt him with some water to cool him down,' Kuseniseni said.

'No, Kuseniseni. That's mean,' I said.

'Who are you talking to, the bird again?' Mwezi asked.

'Yes, I am. He wants the elephant to squirt you with water because he thinks it'll calm you down,' I responded.

'Yeah, right, now who has their head up with the stars?' Mwezi responded.

No sooner had he said it, and Mama Njovu aimed her trunk at Mwezi and squirted him with water. Sofu laughed. At first, Mwezi was shocked, but then he laughed too.

'Wow, I can't read this kid. I didn't see that coming,' Kuseniseni said.

'That was cool! You can *really* talk to animals? Why can't I hear what they're saying?' Mwezi asked.

'Well, I guess it's a gift I have. You know, like you have the gift of always causing trouble. Talking to animals is my gift, but you can't tell anyone! It'll be our secret, okay?' I said, pleading at him with my eyes. I never knew which way things would go with him.

'I promise to keep my mouth shut, but only if you let me come out to play with you,' he responded.

'Deal!' I said, and we gave each other high-fives.

As I was about to introduce Mwezi to the animals, Pululu flew over and said, 'I hate to break up the party, but Pembele needs to talk to you.'

'To talk to me. Why? She doesn't even like me,' I asked.

'Just talk to her, and you'll understand,' Pululu said, then turned to Mama Njovu. 'Hey, Mama, why don't you take the kid for a ride while Pembele talks to his sister? You know, to make up for that little shower you gave him.'

Mama Njovu sashayed over to Mwezi and lowered herself. Before I even explained she wanted to give him a ride, he climbed on her trunk then her back without hesitation.

He grinned from ear to ear. I smiled at him and said I'd be right back. He shouted down at me excitedly, 'Look at me; I'm just like Mowgli!'

I hesitantly walked over to Pembele, and before I could say anything, she said, 'I need you to trust me. Gently place your hand on my horn. Close your eyes, and stay completely still.' It was the first time she spoke to me, so I wasn't sure how to react. Was it some trap or test? I looked over to Pululu, who gave me a reassuring nod. So, I got closer to Pembele and lightly placed my hand on her horn.

'Now, close your eyes, and see with your inner eyes,' Pembele said.

It seemed like a bizarre request. My gut told me it was okay, and Mum always said to trust my feelings. I heard a voice inside me say, *Go ahead; it's okay.* Well, it was more like a feeling than a voice. So, I did as Pemeble asked, not knowing what to expect, but she was calm in a way I hadn't seen before. I closed my eyes and took a couple of deep breaths. Suddenly, I found myself witnessing the scene where Shikulu died and saw everything as it happened. Finally, I understood why Pembele didn't like humans. I also discovered the truth about the way my shikulu died. It wasn't because of a rhinoceros; it was at the hands of evil poachers. I felt sick because the man I saw—the man who was there when Shikulu died and knew the truth about what happened—was staying at the lodge. Everyone fell over themselves trying to please him. He was some kind of VIP guest. I opened my eyes, and for the first time, Pembele and I saw and understood each other. Pembele was lost and looking for answers like I was.

'Pululu! That horrible man there when my shikulu died? He is staying at the lodge!' I shouted.

'Yes. That is why Pembele wanted you to see the truth. We saw him yesterday with the other man, Ngoshe (black mamba snake), the poacher. He was the terrifying one. Like a black mamba, the bullet from his gun is like the snake's venom, lethally dangerous and menacing. They're after Mbwili; we don't know when they're going to get her, but it's soon. They've been tracking her. She bothers us, but she's our problem to deal with, not evil Ngoshe. Mbwili's in trouble and needs our help.'

'I have to tell my mum and Peter. But how? Where would I even start? What if that Ngoshe man also tries to hurt my mum the way he hurt my shikulu?' I said.

Pululu looked at me and said in a sombre voice, 'It's no accident you came here. There was a reason, and now, you know why.'

'You sound like my mum. That's something she would say. She always quotes stuff from some book she's been reading. The words sound so similar. It's like you're both reading from the same book,' I said.

Pululu continued, 'My child, we are all connected. Deep inside, we all know the truth, what's right, and what we need to do. We recognise it; it isn't anything new. It's something we have always had within us. It's like when we hear it or feel it, we remember. You may think you heard it from your mother, but you already knew. It's not by chance you came here, and it's not by chance today's the day Pembele chose to communicate with you, and *you chose to listen*. We don't understand humans, but you do, which is why you will know exactly what to do with the information you have.'

'Let me put it another way. We have a saying, "*isembe talitwa ichitwa mutima*," which means an axe can be blunt when cutting a tree, but if you agree with your heart, you will achieve the goal,' Pululu continued.

'Okay, what you just said made no sense, and yet somehow, I understood what you meant. I know what I should do because the answer is already inside me, right?' I looked at Pululu and remembered a quote my mother always said, 'In quietness, are all things answered.'[15] Mbuyu also had a saying, '*Uwingila mumushitu tomfwa inswaswa,*' which meant: when you're in the thick of the forest, you expect to hear a lot of noise, but it's all noise you can ignore. Our inner voice always reminds us everything else falls into place when we pay attention to what truly matters. I get it now.

Right at that moment, it hit me! It was one of Oprah's lightbulb moments—my mum always watched the Oprah Winfrey show reruns, and sometimes, I watched them with her. I knew what I had to do. As I played back the scene Pembele showed me, I realised I'd let my feelings consume me and hadn't considered the sacrifices my family made to come here. How painful it must have been for my mum and my dad to return here, to be reminded every day how Shikulu died—a person my dad was very close to, someone who was a father figure to him. Now, they had to live through all the pain again but differently once they find out the truth.

Then, there was my little Bug-a-boo. It was hard for him too. Like me, he had to leave what was familiar, and instead of being there for him, I escaped into my own world. He was only trying to get my attention when he bugged and annoyed me.

I looked up and saw Mwezi on Mama Njovu's back. He shrieked with laughter, having the time of his life. Right then and there, I felt a lightness. It was like I had carried this heavy load, and when I let go of the anger, resentment, and blame, I felt brand new. When I closed my eyes and took a deep breath, I knew everything was as it should be. *I am where I should be.* Then, I opened my eyes and had a sense of clarity I couldn't quite put into words; *I just know that I know.* My mum liked to say, 'Truth will correct all errors in your mind.'[16] I never understood what that meant, but I think I understood now.

'Wait a minute! Someone videoed the whole thing. When the commotion happened, he dropped the camera. Did anyone find it? Would anyone know where it could be? Could someone have hidden it? A young boy watched from Shikulu's patrol car, but I don't know who he is. He looks familiar, but I can't place him,' I finally exclaimed.

'Well, if anyone took something, it would have to be the kolwes. The monkeys are always up to mischief; I'll find out and send a message to you through Kuseniseni,' Pululu said.

'Okay, let me know as soon as you can,' I said.

'Come on, Bug-a-boo! We need to get back for breakfast,' I shouted up to my brother, still on Mama Njovu's back.

'Ohhhh! Do we have to leave now? I'm having so much fun!' he yelled back.

'Yes, we do. Come on! And don't fall asleep during online class. You've had quite the adventure this morning!' I said as he slid off Mama Njovu's trunk.

CHAPTER 6
DOING THE RIGHT THING

After class, I found Kuseniseni waiting on the windowsill in my room. I opened the shutters and let him in.

'Pululu asked me to bring you a message. The kolwes said they didn't take the camera. It was the kid there; he took it,' he said.

'That doesn't help me very much. He looked familiar—I recognised him, but I don't know why,' I said.

'Look, kid. I know you don't like talking to your parents about what happened with your shikulu, but maybe Mr P knows who the kid is,' Kuseniseni said.

'Of course! Thanks, you're a genius!' I said.

'Now *that* we can agree on! One more thing, the kolwes told Pululu, that Ngoshe—the evil poacher-man—knows about Pembele. He spotted her tracks a few days ago. The elephants had been careful to step over her tracks but may have missed some. He knows she's here,' Kuseniseni said.

'Oh, no! We need to do something right now,' I said.

'Well, start by talking to Mr P,' Kuseniseni said.

'I'll go and find him right away,' I replied.

'Hey, Princess, wait! Got any food for me?' Pululu shouted.

'Oh, I wasn't expecting you, so I didn't pick up anything from the kitchen,' I responded.

Kuseniseni fluttered towards the windowsill, but I revealed the bunch of mulberries in a paper bag behind me before he got there.

He turned around and opened his eyes even wider than usual (if that's even possible). He pecked away happily at the berries as I headed to Mr P's office.

'Mr P? Are you busy?' I asked as I knocked on his door.

'Miss K. What's up?' he smiled.

'Tell me about how my shikulu died,' I said in a hushed voice.

'What brought this on?' he asked.

'Something about the version I heard doesn't make sense,' I replied.

'In what way?' He looked puzzled.

'Well, from everything I've heard about Shikulu, he was the absolute best at what he did,' I said.

'Yes, he was. The best of the best. Look, I'm not sure if it's my place to say anything,' Mr P responded.

'No one ever talks about it, at least not to me,' I pleaded. 'Please tell me'

'Okay, Miss K.' He looked uneasy. 'Tell me the version you've heard.'

'When he went to rescue a rhino from a trap a poacher had set, the rhino turned on him. He could've shot at it but chose to die rather than kill a rhino,' I said.

'That's pretty much the version I know,' Mr P added.

'But I want to know the details. Why was he alone? When you or my mum investigate these things, you always have back up or one of the dogs from the K-9 unit,' I said.

'Well, for one thing, during your grandfather's time, there was no K-9 unit. He was out on a routine patrol and only had my young brother, Chilufya, with him. From time to time, he snuck into his patrol car, and your shikulu had a soft spot for him. The account I have is from Chilufya. He was only a young boy and very scared,' Peter responded.

So, Chilufya has the camera. 'So, he saw what happened to my shikulu?' I asked Mr P.

'No, your shikulu told him to wait in the car. Chilufya heard the commotion, but he was too afraid to come out of the car. He radioed for help, but by the time we got there, it was too late. But from his account of what he could make out, your shikulu found a rhino in a trap the poachers set for her. When trying to release the rhino, it turned on him, knocked him over, and ran off. Chilufya was very shaken and didn't speak about it for days,' Peter responded.

'Yeah. I guess that's the version drilled in my head too,' I mumbled to myself.

'What happened to the rhino?' I asked.

'Unfortunately, the poachers got to her. We found her the next day with her horns sawn-off. We had been tracking her for some time, but she disappeared for a while. She was pretty much the last remaining rhino in the area, and no one had seen rhinos here since then. We had been tracking her because she was pregnant, but when we found her after the poachers got to her, there was no calf, and she wasn't pregnant anymore. We searched and searched for that calf but never found it. We assumed the poachers must've taken it with them.'

I thought about my new friend. Pembele must've been scared when she lost her mother. She was also lucky she had friends like Pululu, Mama Njovu, and Kuseniseni, who kept her hidden and safe all this time. Pululu told me how Mama Njovu found Pembele and immediately took her under her wing. She fed, protected, and cared for her as a mother would. Mama Njovu was the matriarch, the mother to all. Whatever she said went. So, when she told everyone to hide and protect Pembele from the humans, everyone did it without question. Mama Njovu somehow reminded me of my mbuya; when she talked, everyone listened and did what she asked, even my mother.

But Mama Njovu was worried about Pembele, and I was too. With Ngoshe back, she had to relive it all again. He was not only here for Mbwili; he was after her too. I'm her friend, and she needed my help.

'Mr P, maybe Chilufya didn't tell you the whole story?' I asked.

'What do you mean? Why would you say something like that?' he asked.

'Well, you said my shikulu was the best of the best. It doesn't make sense he wouldn't have been more careful. You also said Chilufya was scared and didn't talk much about it. What if he saw something else that scared him so much he couldn't talk about it?' I said.

'Well, Miss K, I know it's hard to accept. Even I had a hard time believing that happened, but what other explanation could there be?' Peter asked with his hand on his chin.

'Something doesn't add up, and as you said, I have a connection with Shikulu, so maybe I should speak to Chilufya; he might help me understand,' I responded.

'What on earth would Chilufya have to say *now* that he didn't tell us before?' Peter asked.

'Just trust me on this one, Mr P. Did you see how Chilufya panicked when that VIP guest spoke to him?' I said.

'You mean the former councillor? Chilufya didn't panic; he showed respect to someone older and in authority, something you need to learn, young lady!' Mr P said.

'Look, Mr P. I don't know what you think you saw, but Chilufya is afraid of that man,' I replied.

'Okay, Miss K, I don't know what kind of conspiracy theory you cooked up in your head, but I'll ask him to talk to you—if only to stop you from pestering me about this.'

'Thanks, Mr P!'

'Oh, speak of the devil,' Mr P said as Chilufya walked towards Mr P's office.

'Ummm, Chilufya, I know you don't like to talk about this, but Miss K would like to fill in a few gaps about her shikulu's death.'

'Why are we talking about this now? That was so long ago. Is it because the former councillor is here?' Chilufya said, looking uneasy.

'The councillor?' Mr P was intrigued. 'What does he have to do with this?'

'Oh, n-n-n-nothing,' Chilufya said. 'It's just that he was the local councillor when the a-a-a-ccident happened.'

'You remember that?' Mr P asked, looking both surprised and impressed.

'Oh no-no-no-nooooo,' Chilufya stammered again. 'I didn't remember. He mentioned it to me earlier, asking me if he looked familiar to me. I said he didn't. That's when he told me he used to be a regular here when he was the area councillor.'

'See, Miss K, it wasn't fear or panic; he was embarrassed because he didn't recognise him,' Mr P said.

Mr P looked at Chilufya and asked, 'When did your nervous stammer return? I thought it was a thing of the past. Anyway, I'll leave you two to talk.' He shook his head as if he didn't quite understand and left the office.

Chilufya looked at me and said, 'I'm r-r-r-really sorry about your shikulu. How I wish I could tell you more, but it was so long ago; I can't remember.'

'Oh, I think you remember everything—you may be a lot older, but you still have that same scared look now you had all those years ago when you saw what happened,' I said sternly.

It caught Chilufya totally off guard.

'H-H-H-How could you possibly know what ha-ha-ha-happened that day?' he asked.

'My shikulu's ghost told me,' I responded (it was the first thing that came into my mind, and people in this area can be quite superstitious, but it seemed to work).

'Are y-y-y-you b-b-b-being serious right now?' he asked.

'Deadly,' I said with a straight face.

Chilufya looked around the room as if expecting to see my shikulu's ghost suddenly appear.

'Okay, l-l-l-look. At the time, I was only a kid, even younger than you are now. I loved your shikulu; he was the c-c-c-coolest and took me everywhere with him. He did this really neat thing with the animals—it was like they seemed to *listen* to him. I don't know how, but he used some next level jedi-trick to communicate with them. It seemed no one would believe a rhino turned on him because he had a way with the animals. But I was s-s-s-scared. That councillor told me if I told anyone, we would suffer in the same way your shikulu did, so I told them it was an accident. They told me exactly what to say. I'm s-s-s-sorry,' Chilufya said.

'No, I get it. So, what really happened?' I said.

'The truth was when we got to the trapped rhino, your shikulu was in the process of releasing it, but the poachers ambushed him. In the commotion, the poacher shot at the rhino, and the injured rhino accidentally knocked your shikulu over, and he hit his head on a stone. The poachers chased after the injured rhino and left your shikulu. When the coast was clear, I came out of the car, but it was too late. I r-r-r-radioed for help and stayed with him until Peter and your mum came,' Chilufya continued.

Chilufya paused. Then, he continued. 'But one guy took a video of the whole thing. I don't know why, but I heard this particular poacher, Ngoshe, liked to capture all his *trophies—and* how he got them—on camera. When the rhino charged, the guy with the video camera must have panicked and dropped the camera. All the cars drove off quickly because they wanted to catch the rhino. For some reason, I put it in my backpack and never watched it. I was so scared that day; I didn't speak and didn't show anyone the tape.

The next day, the councillor came to the lodge to pay his respects. When Peter told him I was with your shikulu, he asked to speak with me. He told Peter he wanted to offer me words of comfort and asked if I saw or found anything. I told him no. When he asked if I was sure, I told him I remembered some kolwes picking up something and running off with it, but I didn't know what it was. That's when he threatened my family. He said if I *suddenly remembered* anything else and told them what I saw, then the same thing would happen to all of us. Obviously, he and Ngoshe played a part in it, but I was too afraid to say anything. That's why I've been quiet all these years.'

'That's *really* scary. So, I guess when he spoke to you earlier today, he was giving you a friendly reminder?' I said.

'Yeah, s-s-s-something like that. You know what, Kay, not a day passed I didn't think about your shikulu. Now, I guess you know why I avoided you and your parents. But you know what? It's never too late to do the right thing. I'm going to show that tape to Peter and your mum. If the councillor is here, then something bad is about to go down, and this time, I'm not going to sit back and let it happen,' Chilufya said.

As he walked out, I shouted, 'Hey, Chilufya. Thank you!'

He turned and paused for a second and said, 'No, Kay. Thank you.'

I wanted to warn my parents, but it was better if Chilufya and Peter handled it. Still, I felt nervous and scared. *The man was at the lodge; what if he harmed them? What if he didn't believe Chilufya when he said he didn't remember him? What if what happened to Shikulu happens to them? To us?*

I watched as Chilufya went over with the tape and spoke to Mr P and my mum. They headed over to Mr P's office, and my mum called for my dad to join them. *I guess that old VCR in his office was finally good for something.*

They watched the video and saw other footage of the notorious poacher, Ngoshe, meeting up with the councillor, exchanging money. Then, they saw the confrontation with Shikulu and Pembele's mum shot.

My parents and Peter fumed but needed to figure out the best way to catch the poacher and the councillor. I walked into Mr P's office and asked, 'Would it help if I told you the other bad man in the video is here and where they are going to meet? The rumours about the baby rhino are true. Now, the rhino is fully grown, and they've come for her. They think they're the only ones who know about her; they spotted her tracks a few days ago and want to act fast,' I said before my mum could say anything.

'Miss Kay, I'm not even going to ask how you know all of this. Between talking Nyasa birds and all those other animals you're *vibing* with, I know what you're saying is true,' Peter responded.

'Well, you may not need to know, but I need answers! How do you know all this? You saw the most deadly, evil, vile, and nastiest of all the poachers. They call him Ngoshe, because like black mamba, he doesn't discriminate; he attacks anything in his way,' my mum said.

'I'm sorry, Mum. I heard the councillor on the phone, and he called him Ngoshe. He didn't know I was there, but he said they would meet at the Big Baobab tree near the Lupunga Spa before the sunrise safari tomorrow. But I also saw the evil poacher-man meet him in the car park. The councillor told him never to come here again.' Mum looked at me, not quite sure what to make of all this.

'I didn't think you would believe me if I told you what the councillor was up to. Also, I was scared because I thought what happened to Shikulu would happen to you. But they are horrible people and need to stop. Though Shikulu didn't have all the information, now you've seen the video and know everything. You'll know what to do to stop them from hurting other animals,' I told them.

'Kay, what have we told you about eavesdropping? If what you say is true and he noticed you listening, you could've been hurt or even worse,' my dad said.

'Your dad is right. Peter and I are going to check this out, but in the meantime, don't do any more detective work. From now on, I don't want to hear anything from you about councillors or evil poacher-men. Confine yourself to your bedroom and the small kitchen; that's where you'll have your meals until we clear all this up. Oh, and I don't want to hear anything about you disappearing and no one being able to find you! And no, you cannot go to the library to get a WIFI or phone signal. I don't want you talking to anyone!' my mum said.

And with that, she walked away. Peter followed after her and stopped to give me an encouraging or consoling pat on my back. My dad gave me a disapproving look and walked away.

Like I said earlier, *parents are the worst*! Instead of being happy with the information I gave her, my mum had a go at me and punished me. It doesn't make any sense. Now, I can't even see my friends. I'm scared of testing her when she speaks to me with *that* tone. I hope Pembele will be okay.

I don't even know if I'll see Kuseniseni in the morning. Mbuya arrives on the early morning flight tomorrow, so we have to leave for the airport way before the ngoma beats. She's only staying for a few days because it's my birthday, and she never misses it. She's the only one who gets me. I can't wait to see her and hear about Zozo and everything back home. *I wonder if she and Kai saw each other at all since we left.*

REFLECTION

Have you ever been in a situation where you thought you knew the whole story but then found out the version of the story you know wasn't completely accurate? If you found out the truth and knew sharing this truth would help other people—even if it meant putting them through pain—what would you do? This part has been deliberately left blank for you to write down your thoughts.

PART 6
RECOGNITION

Recognition *noun (knowing)*

the act of remembering who somebody is when you see them, or of identifying what something is[17]

the fact of knowing someone or something because you have seen or heard her or him, or experienced it before[18]

CHAPTER 7
THIS IS ME!

The drive to the airport was quiet—no Peter, no Mum, just Dad, Mwezi, and Friday (one of the guides). Mwezi teased him and called him whatever day of the week it was. Ironically, today his name was Friday because it is Friday. Everyone at the lodge did it, so they kept track of the days of the week by asking Friday his name each day.

I hadn't seen my mum or Peter since last night. We left early for the airport. My mum usually wished me a happy birthday first in some goofy way, and I acted like I thought it was lame. But truthfully, I always looked forward to her birthday surprises. Somehow, she got me when I least expected it. But today, I told myself the only reason she hadn't wished me a happy birthday was because she had to catch Ngoshe and the councillor in action. But a part of me felt it was because she was still mad at me for *eavesdropping* on the councillor.

I wondered if my mum and Peter got to the baobab tree in time to stop the evil poacher-man. *What if something happened to them?*

When I asked my dad about them, he told me not to worry about things I had no business worrying about. I hadn't even seen Kuseniseni that morning. At least he would have heard or seen something and told me what was going on.

Some birthday it was turning out to be. The drive to the airport was long, and I hadn't slept much, worrying about my mum and Peter. My eyes got heavy, and I decided to rest for a bit until we got to the airport.

Mbuya's voice singing happy birthday to me woke me. When I fell asleep, no one woke me up when we arrived at the airport. I opened my eyes, and my grandma stood before me with oversized dark sunglasses and a large, wide-brimmed straw hat on her head. She removed the mask from her face and mumbled something like, 'I'm so used to wearing this thing; I forget to take it off.'

'There's my Ray,' she said. (She calls me Ray in part because of my name and also because she said I'm the first ray of sun-shine since Shikulu passed away.)

'Mbuya! Why didn't anyone wake me up?' I squealed as I got out of the minivan and rushed to hug her.

Before my dad could answer, Mwezi sang, *'Walala, Washala!'* which basically meant, 'you snooze, you lose.'

'Happy birthday, Ray!' my grandma said.

'Thank you, Mbuya,' I said while still in her embrace.

'How does it feel to be a teenager? Let me have a look at you. You're all grown up! You don't look thirteen; you could pass for fifteen! What have you been eating out here? I thought you would be all skin and bones, but it looks like you've settled in nicely.' Then, she took her right thumb, licked her tongue with it, and before I knew it, she wiped the *manongo* (sleep) from my eyes.

'Mbuya, I'm not a baby anymore; you could've just told me to wipe my eyes with a tissue,' I said.

'You're still my little Ray!' she responded with a huge smile on her face.

I hugged her one more time. 'Did you see Kai before you left? How was he?' I asked.

'Well, why don't you ask him yourself?' she tapped the send button on her phone and handed it to me.

'Happy birthday Kay Kay,' a voice said from the phone; she had him on video chat.

I screamed, 'Kai!'

'There's no way I was going to miss giving you a birthday wish for your first birthday in the bush. Us teenagers need to look out for each other!' Kai turned thirteen before we left for the bush.

'It's so good to see your face! Are you in the car? Where are you going?' I said.

'Happy birthday, Kay Kay. We're taking a little road trip; it's not the same without you,' Kai's parents said.

'Aww, thank you. Where are you off to?' I said.

'Kay Kay, I'll try and call you a little later.' The signal was glitchy.

'Sorry, Ray. He asked me to video call as soon as I was with you since the lodge's phone signal was so bad. At least you got to see each other,' Mbuya said.

'I guess so. It was great to see his face and hear his voice. Thank you, Mbuya,' I responded.

'Okay. Let's get you in the car; we've got a long drive ahead of us. You can ask all those questions on the drive to the lodge,' my father said.

Mbuya and I sat in the back row. Dad and Mwezi sat in the row closest to the driver's seat. Friday loaded the luggage, and we started the long drive back to the lodge. Mbuya told us all about everyone back home and how naughty Zozo still was. 'There's no teaching that dog any manners!' she pretended to complain.

I asked Mbuya if she heard about the latest drama with Ngoshe and the councillor. 'We're not talking about that,' my father shouted from the front. Mbuya and I talked in hushed voices. She told me how she spoke to Mum before she boarded her flight. Mum told her all about the councillor and evil poacher-man and how they were linked to an international money-laundering ring. She explained how money launderers used money from illegal businesses—like poaching—and *cleaned* it by putting it through legal businesses, so the people laundering the money didn't get caught and thrown into prison. It all sounded complicated and a lot of effort and trouble to clean money when *you could just get a job*. But grown-ups do the strangest things.

'What are you two whispering about back there?' my dad asked.

'Oh, nothing, Dad! Just talking about Zozo,' I replied.

'I bet she's telling Mbuya how she talks to animals,' Mwezi said as I cut my eyes at him. He covered his mouth with both his hands when he realised he broke his promise to me and may never get another ride on Mama Njovu.

'Your shikulu used to think he could talk to the animals,' Mbuya said, and everyone chuckled.

Mbuya and I chatted halfway to the lodge, and she fell asleep.

I started to think about everything and told myself Mum and Peter would be home when we arrived and could tell us everything.

When we got to the lodge, my mum and Peter were still not back. My dad didn't seem worried; he was deep in discussions with Mbuya (who was wide awake) about all the family drama in Lusaka.

I rushed to my room, hoping to find Kuseniseni there, but there was no sign of him, which worried me. Mum and Peter should've been back. I wondered why we hadn't heard anything.

My dad walked into my room and sat at the edge of my bed.

'Kay, I know this isn't the start you were expecting for your birthday, but I just got off the phone with your mum—' he said.

'Is she okay?' I interrupted before he could finish. 'Did they catch the poacher-man?' I asked before he could respond.

'Well, she didn't go into any details but asked I tell you she didn't mean to snap at you last night. She wants you to enjoy your day without worrying about what she's doing. We'll take Mbuya on a sunset game drive, and your mum will join us for your birthday dinner afterwards,' he said.

'But . . .' I said.

'No *buts*, Kay. Your mum is fine. There are a few formalities she needs to take care of at the town office, so she'll be out for most of the day. Why don't you go for a swim with your brother before we have brunch?' my dad said.

He left the room, and I wanted to rush to the watering hole to see if any of the animals could tell me anything about what happened at the baobab tree and if Pembele was safe. But it was already mid-morning and especially hot. They'd probably already left and were sheltering under Mahogany trees across the Valley—Pululu called them natural air conditioners. The animals usually hung out there on really hot days. I supposed even if I did know where to find them, I wouldn't be able to go since my mum said I could not pull any disappearing acts until they caught Ngoshe.

I spent the rest of the day lounging by the pool with Mwezi, Dad, and Mbuya. I didn't swim because the universe decided to surprise me with a birthday present. My first period appeared. Luckily, my mum had already talked me through it and made me watch 101 YouTube videos about what to expect and what to do. She already bought a tonne of sanitary towels, so I was well prepared. Dad kept asking why I wasn't swimming—I was usually the first to jump into the pool. I didn't share my news with him because I promised Mum when '*aunt Flo*' finally arrived, she would be the first person to know.

Dad and Mbuya kept disappearing, and I spotted them suspiciously whispering with Friday. At first, I thought it's about my mum, but then, of course, Mwezi—the keeper of all secrets—told me they were planning my birthday surprise.

'It can't be much of a surprise. We're having dinner after the game drive,' I said.

I wasn't really in the mood for a game drive, but Mbuya was excited about it and said she wouldn't go if I didn't go. So, I guess we had to go on a game drive, and they probably needed me out of the way at the lodge to plan my birthday *surprise.*

For the game drive, we jumped into the open-sided 4x4 (Toyota) Land Cruiser. I loved sitting at the back because with the tiered seating, that was the highest part, but my mum didn't like me sitting there because it was also the bumpiest part. I heaved myself up on the step in the middle row, and my dad said, 'Come on, Kay. Since it's your birthday, you can sit wherever you like.'

I looked at him, not sure whether he was serious. Mum was quite militant about me and Mwezi not sitting in the back, and he never disagreed with her.

'Go on. I know you want to sit in the back,' he said.

'Thanks, Dad!' I said and jumped into the middle of the back seat so Mwezi didn't get any ideas about joining me.

'I wanted to sit in the back too!' Mwezi said in protest.

'No, not you. You're sitting in the middle row with Mbuya,' my dad said.

He reluctantly sat next to Grandma in the middle row, and Dad sat in the front next to Friday.

'No spotter today?' I asked.

My dad hesitated, then responded, 'I'll be your spotter today.'

About an hour into the game drive, Friday received a call on his radio and stopped the vehicle. He turned around and looked at us thoughtfully. He said something to my dad, who nodded his head in agreement, then Friday spoke to the rest of us.

'I just received a call about a dangerous poacher in the park, and they need an extra pair of hands to help catch him.'

My worst fears came true, and I understood why my mum and Peter had been out all day. The poacher-man got away.

'An extra pair of hands—what does that mean?' Mbuya asked.

'It means I'm going to park the vehicle somewhere safe and join the rest of the team tracking the poacher. You will all stay in the vehicle until I get back,' Friday responded.

'That doesn't sound right. You can't leave us alone. What if the poacher comes and kidnaps us?' Mbuya said.

I felt frightened because I saw what that man did.

Mwezi was quiet but hugged Mbuya tightly.

'Look, Mfuwe Lodge is nearby. Friday, you can leave us there and go ahead and join the tracking team,' my dad said.

'Okay, let me radio them to let them know we are taking a detour to Mfuwe Lodge,' Friday said.

I kept looking around, hoping I'd see Kuseniseni or Pululu or any of the animals who could tell me where Ngoshe was so I could tell Friday which direction to find him, but none of them were anywhere in sight.

As we approached Mfuwe Lodge, there seemed to be quite a bit of commotion. I'd been there a few times with my mum and had never seen it so busy.

'We have to be quick,' Friday said.

'I can't believe you were going to leave us out in the bush alone,' Mbuya said to Friday.

Before Friday had a chance to respond, I heard the happy birthday chorus led by a very familiar voice. But it couldn't be; I just spoke to him this morning! I turned my head and saw Kai with his parents, singing happy birthday to me.

'Kai!' I screamed, still not quite sure he was there.

'In the *byu-byu!*'[19] he responded, quoting a line from our favourite song. We both started singing, *'Ah Nde Twah by Chanda na Kay*[20] while dancing to our modified version of the Toosie Slide.[21]

I was so happy to see Kai; we abruptly ended our dance and gave each other a big hug.

'I thought you were acting a bit weird on the video chat,' I said to him. 'I can't believe you've been here the whole time.'

'*Mmmmmmm, you skeem*[22] *I can miss out on your birthday butah?'*[23] he responded. '*So apa here you want to perform, ka!*'[24]

Before I could reply, my dad's uncontrollable laugh distracted me. He explained the surprise and how they planned the radio call. But Mbuya, who was in on the surprise, didn't have all the details and completely fell for the whole run-away poacher story. It took all my dad's will power to stop himself from laughing. So, it turned out my mum and Peter *did* capture Ngoshe. Kai and his parents planned to stay at our lodge, but with all the developments, Mum thought it would be a great surprise to have my birthday dinner at Mfuwe Lodge and have Kai and his parents meet us there.

'Where is Mum?' I asked.

'She's inside. There's a press briefing about the capture of the notorious Ngoshe and the arrest of the councillor. They were supposed to have finished by now, but it started late,' Friday responded.

'Come on. Let's go get your mum,' my dad said.

We walked into the conference room where Mum stood at the front, talking about the arrests. She said something about their link to an international money laundering ring and told people in the other countries to follow the money to catch the others. Mum looked up at me, smiled, and said, 'Come up here, Bug. You're the reason this is possible.'

I looked to my dad and Mbuya, who both gave me reassuring nods. So, I walked towards the podium, and Mum met me halfway and bent down to hug me and said, 'Happy birthday, Inspector Kay! Are you okay with talking to the press? I told them how great you were in helping us catch these bad guys.'

I smiled and nodded. She went back to the podium and spoke into the microphone. 'Just a couple of questions; we have a birthday dinner to get to.'

My mum handed me the microphone. I felt a little nervous and looked ahead and saw Mr P give me a thumbs up. Kusenseni and Pululu perched on the ledge of the window. I knew their facial expressions didn't change, but I knew deep inside they were smiling. So, I cleared my throat and spoke into the microphone.

'Before you ask me any questions, I have something to say.' I looked up, and Mbuya, Mum, and Kai smiled with pride. I had no idea what to say but trusted in my inner guidance as I remembered Pululu's words about how we always have an inner knowing and have to be still and listen.

'People think of the animals in the bush like they are wild and do things without thinking, yet it's the *people* who behave like they are wild and untamed animals. It's people who poach the animals and burn the trees with no regard for the consequences. **Humans** kill the animals and collect their skins and other parts to sell for the money they think will last forever. Animals understand abundance and know how to meet their daily needs. They flow with nature's cycle, but humans mess with the natural order of things. Animals understand the divine order in everything, but humans claim to be superior and disturb this order. We need to give nature a chance and reinstate a natural order if we give nature a chance. That's all I wanted to say.'

Suddenly, everyone stood up and clapped.

Then, a reporter said, 'Those are wise words from such a young girl. I suppose you learned this from your mum?'

'Well, some of it, I guess. But the animals told me most of it,' I responded.

There was shocked silence and then a murmur. I looked up at Mr P, who had a big smile on his face. Then, I looked up at the window, and Kuseniseni looked like his head was about to explode. Pululu looked calm as always and nodded her head in approval.

I paused for a bit, chuckled, and said, 'I'm just kidding; animals can't talk.'

'You had us going for a minute. That's quite the sense of humour you've got,' the reporter said.

I looked up and smiled and said, 'Thank you, next!'

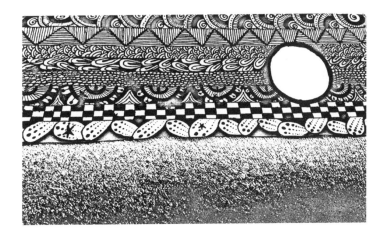

AFTERWARD—SUNSET SAFARI

Tested by discovering her inner strength, Kasuba overcame her fear, embraced her true self, and saved the day through a remarkable journey of self-discovery.

On a game safari, many of you witness the same thing but have completely different experiences. All experiences are unique, like in life's safari. These differences don't mean we should label our journeys and experiences as good or bad. When you exchange stories after a safari, you gain different perspectives and look at things from someone else's perspective. There's more than one way to look at something or experience something, and that's okay. Each method has its merit.

When you look closely at Kasuba's safari, you'll see the journey she took reflects the various paths you will take at different stages in your life. You'll realise you constantly evolve, and change isn't a matter of *if*, but *when*. It's up to you to choose how long you will dwell in the different Rs before you get to the stage of recognising your true self and shine your spotlight on you. Remember, you have an inner guide who will direct you to where you want to go. In a world where you want to be anything, be yourself.

GLOSSARY / DICTIONARY

Ah Nde Twah	A song by Zambian Hip Hop Duo – Chanda na Kay
Apa	Here
Bally	Father or a man who could be a father, not necessarily your own
BFF	Best Friend Forever
Buta	Friend or brother (has origins from the Afrikaans word for mate or chum – boet)
Byu-byu	Building (as in in the building – in the byu-byu)
Chanda na Kay	A Zambian Hip Hop Duo
Chibanda	Ghost
Chitenge	Fabric used as a harness to hold baby
Dip	Leave or go
DSTV	Digital Satellite Television
Eksay	Friend / mate / buddy
Ichifu	Tripe
Iwe	You
Ka	Right?
Kasuba	Sun
Kolwe	Monkey
Kuseniseni	Very early in the morning
Lupili	Hill
Lutanda	Star
Manongo	Sleep (the gooey stuff that you see at the corners of your eyes when you wake up in the morning)

Matebeto	A traditional ceremony which is part of the marriage rites
Mayo	Mother
Mbuya	Grandmother
Mfuwe	A town in Zambia's Eastern Province
Muzungu	Caucasian / white person
Mwana	Baby or friend
Mwezi	Moon
Ngoma	Drum
Ngoshe	Black Mamba (snake)
Ohn	A person (usually a guy)
Perf or Perform	Dramatic
Pick n Pay	A South African supermarket chain
Safari	A trip to photograph & observe animals in their natural habitat (also a journey in Swahili)
Saht	No
Salaula	Secondhand clothing for sale
Savannah	A grassy plain
Shikulu	Grandfather
Shoprite	A South African supermarket chain
Skeem	Think
Spar	A South African supermarket chain
Tata	Father
Tuning	Saying / talking
VCR	Video Cassette Recorder

BIBLIOGRAPHY

Dictionary.cambridge.org. 2020. *Cambridge English Dictionary: Meanings & Definitions.* [online] Available at: https://dictionary.cambridge.org/dictionary/english/

Oxfordlearnersdictionaries.com. 2020. *Oxford Advanced Learner's Dictionary At Oxford Learner's Dictionaries | Find Meanings And Definitions Of Words.* [online] Available at: https://www.oxfordlearnersdictionaries.com/definition/english/

1977. *A Course In Miracles.* New York, N.Y.: Foundation for Inner Peace.

ENDNOTES

1 A Course in Miracles – Workbook – Part 1 – Lesson 169
2 (rumination noun - Definition, pictures, pronunciation and usage notes | Oxford Advanced Learner's Dictionary at OxfordLearnersDictionaries.com, 2020)
3 (Grande, Ariana, "Thank you, next" 2019)
4 Slang term loosely translated means not what you're saying old man or father
5 (resistance noun - Definition, pictures, pronunciation and usage notes | Oxford Advanced Learner's Dictionary at OxfordLearnersDictionaries.com, 2020)
6 Slang used by Zambian kids, meaning someone is being dramatic (perf is short for performer)
7 Slang meaning no way, or just no
8 A slang term used in Zambia to describe a person, usually a guy
9 A slang term used in Zambia, meaning I have to go
10 A slang term used in Zambia, usually means one's father or a man who could be a father, not necessarily your own
11 (BECOMING AWARE) (REALIZATION | meaning in the Cambridge English Dictionary, 2020)
12 (reassessment noun - Definition, pictures, pronunciation and usage notes | Oxford Advanced Learner's Dictionary at OxfordLearnersDictionaries.com, 2020)
13 Direct translation 'Um, you also'
14 (rediscovery noun - Definition, pictures, pronunciation and usage notes | Oxford Advanced Learner's Dictionary at OxfordLearnersDictionaries.com, 2020)
15 A Course in Miracles – Chapter 27 – IV. The Quiet Answer

[16] A Course in Miracles – Workbook – Part 1 – Lesson 107

[17] (recognition noun - Definition, pictures, pronunciation and usage notes | Oxford Advanced Learner's Dictionary at OxfordLearnersDictionaries.com, 2020)

[18] (RECOGNITION | meaning in the Cambridge English Dictionary, 2020)

[19] Slang term, meaning building

[20] A song by Zambian hip hop duo, Chanda na Kay

[21] A song with an accompanying dance by Canadian rapper Drake from his commercial mixtape *Dark Lane Demo Tapes* (2020).

[22] A slang term used in Zambia, meaning 'think'

[23] A slang term used in Zambia meaning friend or brother (has origins from the Afrikaans word for mate or chum – boet)

[24] Loosely translated the sentence means 'So right now, I bet you want to start being dramatic, right?'

ISQ

Inner Safari Quest (ISQ) is a coaching programme designed specifically for children aged seven–sixteen. ISQ is a unique system using stories like Kasuba's and the Adventures in WISDOM™ system to teach growth mind-set skills in a way children understand. Through a thought-provoking and creative process, children learn critical life skills for developing soaring self-esteem and unstoppable self-confidence, so they can live a life of purpose, happiness, and success while overcoming challenges such as fear, self-doubt, and disappointment. They develop specific skills sets to build emotional intelligence, learn to cope with change, and how to manage mistakes, failures, and peer pressure. Children learn to navigate through life confidently and accept themselves and others for who they are.

SERVICES PROVIDED

PERSONAL COACHING: Individual one on one/Coaching sessions/Face-to-face or online/Tailor made packages/

Self-discovery/Personal Development and Empowerment/ Boost your self-esteem and confidence/Transform limiting beliefs.

GROUP COACHING: Group size of four–ten children/ similar age groups/face to face/Personal Discovery/Personal Development and Empowerment/Boost self-esteem and confidence/Transform limiting beliefs.

EMPOWERING ONE DAY SEMINARS: To encourage personal growth that transforms your life to go from where you are to where you want to be with the guidance of a qualified Life Coach.

CREATIVE SPACES: Safari workshops/retreats on specific topics or themes/Building Resilience/Self-esteem/Self-confidence/ Standing up to peer pressure/Creating your vision board for success.

FACILITATION: Design, organise, and facilitate conferences, workshops, seminars, and away days for schools, and other children's groups.

Experience your own Inner Safari Quest:

www.innersafariquest.com

 InnerSafariQuest_ISQ

 @SafariInner

 Inner-Safari-Quest

ABOUT THE AUTHOR

Born in Lusaka, Zambia and educated in England, Bwalya is a certified Adventures in Wisdom™ Coach. She teaches children how to thrive as they navigate their way through life. She is very passionate about coaching children to become the best that they can be, to be their real selves, and to create the life they desire!

As a child, Bwalya spent a lot of holidays going on Safari to the South Luangwa National Park with her parents and two brothers. She carried on this tradition with her daughter, Chichi-Rene, and goes on safari with her at least once a year. When Bwalya was eight years old, a young rhinoceros wandered onto the airstrip at Mfuwe airport and the flight could not take off for more than hour, until the rhinoceros finally wandered off. Without knowing it, Bwalya felt a connection with that rhinoceros. Shortly after, Bwalya was in a production at her primary school to raise funds to support wildlife conservation in the Luangwa Valley. Bwalya performed a song at this concert, and it still sticks with her today. It goes something like this:

Sunrise over Luangwa Valley, creatures
stir and begin their day.
One appears and the trees all tremble, it's
a young rhinoceros out to play.
There's a one-tonne, two-horned giant in the sun,
It's a three-toed, four-legged rhino on the run.
For he's all too rare, so do take care,
To shoot him with a camera and never with a gun.

Bwalya's mission statement is: '*Just Be*, because being who you are is all that really matters.'

This is Bwalya's first book, which she plans to turn into a series, so look out for more Inner Safari Quests in the near future.